E. A. Owen

Suffocating Secrets

Suffocating Secrets

Suffocating Secrets

Tragic Mercy Book II

E. A. Owen

Twisted Karma Publishing

Suffocating Secrets: Tragic Mercy Book II
Copyright © 2019 by Twisted Karma Publishing.

Cover Design: Matt Seff Barnes (United Kingdom)

Author Website: eaowenbooks.com
Facebook.com/eaowenbooks

ISBN 978-1-7322985-3-8 (Amazon-Paperback)
ISBN 978-1-7322985-7-6 (IngramSpark-Paperback)
ISBN 978-1-7322985-5-2 (eBook-EPUB)
ISBN 978-1-7322985-4-5 (eBook-MOBI)

For My Parents

Who did an amazing job raising me,
and supporting my dreams.
Thank You.
I Love You Both.

Suffocating Secrets

E. A. Owen

PROLOGUE

I quickly glance behind me, breathing heavy, my legs burning from running so fast, adrenaline pumping through my veins. I trip and crack my knee on an overgrown root protruding from the forest ground. The pain radiates through my leg as I scream. I clasp a hand over my mouth, eyes darting frantically. I stumble to my feet. Sharp rocks and dry leaves crunch under my torn-up bare feet, leaving a trail of warm blood behind me. My heart pounds so hard I can hear it echoing in my skull. I had to stop, take a break for just a moment to catch my breath. My throat is dry and scratchy from gasping for air. I frantically look around, my eyes wide with fear. The darkness plays tricks on me. A shadow darts behind a nearby tree, startling me. I gasp, holding my breath as I fight the impulse to turn around. My heart pounds fiercely; my hands clench into a fist, ready to attack my predator. Fear tortures my thoughts, my stomach twisting into a violent cramp. A loud crash paralyzes my soul. I try to run, but my legs are heavy, making it nearly impossible. The shadow darts from behind the tree, charging at me with a machete. I release a curdling scream.

Suffocating Secrets

8

THE CURSE
(TREVOR)

It's been five years since the curse on Aaron Kosminski's blood relatives has been broken. Our lives changed tremendously, to our advantage. All the catastrophes dissipated and faded away, only leaving memories and emotional scaring in its place. I truly feel a curse of karma and justice had manipulated my fate.

My great-great-grandfather, Aaron Kosminski—aka Jack the Ripper—had never been punished for his crimes, therefore corrupting the lives of all those born of him, until five years ago when my great aunt, Angel, broke the curse by reciting a spell during a new moon at midnight while burning sage. I know this may sound crazy to you, but the curse was real, and it directly affected our family for generations. But once Angel had broken the curse, everything changed for the better.

First, Isabella's recovery even baffled her surgeon, Dr. Stevens, who has been performing heart-transplant surgeries for over thirty years and boasts an amazing reputation. He stated that he had never seen anyone recover as quickly as Isabella in his entire career and stressed how lucky we were because so many things could have seriously gone wrong, especially whereas Isabella's donor was an adult male and she was a five-year-old girl, sharing a rare blood type, AB-.

Second, Angel miraculously recovered from Alzheimer's dementia, which progressively had become much worse before the curse had been broken. A specialist performed a series of brain scans, neuropsychological tests, and clinical assessments. The tests all returned negative. The once-progressive degeneration of blood cells a PET scan had detected now radically restored her brain cells to complete health.

Third, my grandmother, Mary, no longer suffers from chronic insomnia. She gets a full eight hours of sleep a night, only waking periodically. As a result, her health has improved immensely with five years of good sleep, which she lost for forty years of her life.

Fourth, I, Trevor, could not forgive myself for committing the greatest sin imaginable then continuing with my life.

Life has treated us good for the last five years. My mom still has not consumed a drop of alcohol and has kept off her weight. My parents' relationship is blossoming every year. They are like little love birds and are happier than ever.

***

Isabella is ten years old, and I've finally decided to date again. I've endured ten years without a female companion, and I'm going a little crazy. The only thing I'm afraid of is Isabella's reaction with having another woman here. Even though she never met her mother, who died during childbirth, we do talk about her often.

I still have not told her the truth about her mother's identity, but I think she's still too young to comprehend the complexity of the situation. Besides, I've been talking myself out of it over the years—somethings are better off unknown. I don't want her thinking any less of me, of her deceased mother, or of herself over something we were completely unaware of.

Discovering how I had been conceived was difficult for me to wrap my head around. No one wants to know they are a product of rape and were given up for adoption. I don't want my daughter having the same disturbing thoughts that have consumed my mind throughout the years. I want to do everything possible to protect her from the truth.

From the outside looking in, I'm sure we seem like a very dysfunctional family with deep, dark secrets. But, honestly, we are happy and trying to move on with our lives after all the catastrophes we have endured.

Life is finally simple, and I don't want to complicate things.

FIRST DATE
(TREVOR)

I haven't been this nervous in fifteen years. I felt sweat dripping down my forehead as I frantically paced back and forth. I haven't held a conversation with another woman besides family in over ten years.

"Women are attracted to confidence," I repeated out loud, as if I could magically transform into a confident stud right before my very eyes.

I glanced in the mirror, noticing the crow's feet wrinkles when I smiled. I stand at 6'2" with an athletic build, square jaw, and dark-haired crewcut. I have narrow green eyes, a roman nose, and thin lips. I've been told that I'm very handsome. Just wish my confidence matched my looks.

Who am I kidding? I'm a thirty-one-year-old single father with a lot of baggage. Who is going to want to date me? I rolled my eyes; I needed to stop torturing myself.

Amber seemed like a nice lady. She's a twenty-six-year-old kindergarten teacher. I met her online through a dating website. I suspected she must love kids if she had become a teacher and must have a lot of patience to teach five- and six-year-olds. Hopefully she looks as good as her pictures. I shouldn't really care about her looks, but let's be honest. It's the first thing we notice about someone.

We'd been chatting online and talking on the phone for three months now, and we decided it was time to finally meet. We're getting together at 7 p.m. at Jonathan's—a nice restaurant on the edge of town I've never been; a work friend had suggested the place. He said it's pricey but a nice place and has great food. Besides, I really enjoy trying new places, and Amber said she had never been there either, so it will be a first for both of us.

The palms of my hands sweated, and I wiped them on my pants. I glanced at the clock on the other side of the room—6:12. I took one last look in the mirror. "You've got this," I said with more confidence in my voice this time.

I drove Isabella to my parents. She was much quieter than normal tonight.

"Is everything okay, Isabella?" I asked concerned as I glanced in the rearview at Isabella sitting in the back seat, gazing out the window in silence.

"Dad, I'm fine," Isabella said annoyed.

"I just want to make sure you're not upset with me."

"Dad! I told you, I'm fine."

"Well, you certainly don't sound it, sweetie. Is something bothering you?"

Bella let out a big sigh. I figured I better just drop it. We both sat in silence the rest of the way to my parents' house. I barely had time to put the car in Park, and Bella jumped out the door and ran inside. I glanced at the time on the car radio—6:36.

I better make this quick, or I'm going to be late for my first date.

I jogged to the front door, knocked and let myself in. My parents both stood from the dining room table and approached me.

"Dad. Mom. Sorry to take off so quick, but I'm running a little behind. Bella seems off tonight. See if you can find out what's bothering her. She won't tell me anything. I think she might be mad at me for going on a date."

"Don't worry about Bella. She'll be just fine. Go have fun for once in your life. You deserve it!" Dad said with a smile as he ushered me out the door and closed the door behind me.

I couldn't help but worry about Bella during the ride to Jonathan's. My entire world revolved around her, and I hate seeing her upset. But, like Dad has told me time after time, I just need to do things for myself sometimes and that Bella is no longer a little kid. Which is true. She'll be a teenager in just a couple years.

I shook my head, expelling the negative thoughts so I could enjoy the evening with Amber.

I pulled into the packed parking lot. A few cars waited in line for valet service.

Good thing I made reservations a couple weeks ago. It would've been embarrassing if we showed up and couldn't get seated.

My eyes scanned the parking lot for an empty space. I pulled behind the other cars waiting for valet. I would never find a parking spot in this circus.

A gentleman approached my car as I exited, and I handed him my keys. As I headed toward Jonathan's front entrance, I tried walking with more confidence as I tugged my shirt, hoping I had dressed nice enough. I wore a nice pair of designer dark-colored jeans with a white polo. I always thought white looked nice on me in contrast against my tan skin tone. I just hope I don't make a fool of myself and spill something on it while I'm eating. White was probably a bad choice.

While I approached the host stand, my gaze wandered, admiring the sophisticated ambience—a much fancier place than I'm used to. I tugged my collar and cleared my throat. "Reservation for Trevor Williams."

"The reservation is for two. Shall I seat you or would you like to wait at the bar for the other guest to arrive?" the attractive, tall, slender young lady with blond hair asked with a smile, revealing two cute dimples.

"I'll just wait at the bar. Thank you."

I ordered a drink, hoping it would calm my nerves. They call it *liquid courage* for a reason.

I glanced toward the host stand every few minutes, looking for Amber. I peeked at my watch—7:17. I checked my phone to see if Amber had tried calling or texting to tell me she was running late, but nothing.

I noticed a girl at the other side of the bar peering my way. She tried to be subtle, but she was pretty obvious. Every time I glanced at her, she looked away quickly. Her stares made me feel uncomfortable. She was a much bigger girl, pretty face, but she had to be close to three hundred pounds.

I grew impatient and shifted in my seat a few times. My drink was almost empty. I was more nervous than I thought. *I better pace myself. I don't want to be one of those guys who makes a fool of himself by being intoxicated on the first date. I'll give her until 7:30, then I'll try calling her.*

The girl across the bar stood and tripped, almost falling into another table before catching her balance.

I chuckled. *Looks like she had a few too many.*

I ordered another drink. My phone buzzed in my pocket, and I checked the screen—Amber.

"Hi, Amber. Where are you?"

"Trevor, I'm so sorry to do this to you, but I'm not feeling so well. I hoped the nausea would subside, but it's only getting worse. I should have called you sooner. Sorry for making you wait. Can we reschedule our date?"

"Sure. No problem. Hope you feel better," I replied, hoping not to sound disappointed.

"Thanks, Trevor. I feel horrible. Maybe we can meet up sometime next week if you're free?"

"I should be able to work something out. I'll keep in touch. Have a good night, Amber."

"Good night, Trevor."

I hung up, let out a big sigh and chugged my drink. *No need to pace myself now.*

I paid my bill and left. I stopped at a Burger King drive-thru and grabbed a Whopper and fries for the ride home. Even though I'd only had two drinks, I didn't want to risk it with Bella in the car with me, so I crashed at my parents and slept in my childhood room for the night.

***

Rain beating on the window woke me from a sound sleep as a wave of disappointment swept over me, more that she had left me waiting at the restaurant than with her cancelling. She could have at least given me a heads up before I had dropped off Bella at my parents.

My parents claimed Bella would not leave her room the whole night. She had locked herself in her room and refused to talk to either of my parents or unlock the door, which is unlike her. She loves spending time at my parents. They usually play Monopoly or Clue together or watch a movie with popcorn. But, apparently, Bella wanted to be alone.

During the twenty-minute drive home, Bella didn't say a word. I tried talking to her, but she wouldn't look in my direction, leaving me to the millions of thoughts that invaded my head, full of worry and confusion. When we pulled into the driveway at home, she slammed the car door, rocking the car back and forth, then ran inside the house. I decided to give Bella some space since prying just made her angrier with me.

I didn't hear footsteps from upstairs, so I glanced to the backyard and saw Bella climbing the ladder to her treehouse, twelve feet off the ground. Dad had helped me custom build it when she was five. We made the walls from knotty pine and cut out plenty of windows for a great view of the lake. We installed a living area with a pullout couch, a coffee table, and a wall-mounted TV. A desk sits in the corner alongside a small table with two folding chairs, a mini fridge to store beverages, and a snack cabinet. All it was missing was a bathroom. Bella loved her treehouse. She would spend more time there than she did her own bedroom. We called it her "very own private little hideaway." As massive as our house was, she'd rather sit alone in her treehouse.

Isabella didn't have many close friends, which I found odd. I supposed I didn't have many friends growing up either, but, man, that girl loved to read. She owned so many books that I renovated an extra room into a library. It would be as if she transported into another realm and lost touch with reality when she read. She poured herself into the pages while her thoughts absorbed into a deep trance. She had an eighth-grade reading level in fourth grade.

Isabella was a very smart girl—sometimes too smart for her own good.

LIES
&
DECEPTION
(TREVOR)

I never in a million years would have thought Amber was lying to me all along. After trying to meet up with her four more times in three months, she finally came clean with me. I was pretty upset and felt like she was just playing me. I guess this wasn't the first time she had done this to an innocent guy before. She claimed men are all just looking for a trophy to show off on their arm and personality means absolutely zilch to them. She shot off at the mouth, accusing me of being superficial, and threatened to expose men like me.

Her accusations stung. I'm a nice guy, but I don't like being lied to, especially for six months. By starting a dating relationship with deceptive lies, one walked a very thin line—bound to lose balance, faceplant and look like a complete idiot. I wished Amber the best of luck, but I'm not interested. She would continue hurting the men she deceived and hurting herself even more in the process. No one could expect a relationship to last if it started with lies.

After ten years without a female companion and my first online dating experience was what they refer to as being *catfished*, my guard was up. It would be hard to trust someone again. I've heard the horror stories, but I never expected to be a victim. I can see why some people refuse to date anyone online.

To be honest, I don't know how someone would react when I tell them about Julia. They might run for the hills. I must accept the fact that it could be a deal breaker for some people. The hardest part of it all was knowing the right time to divulge the information. I don't want to wait too long and be emotionally attached. But, on the other hand, I don't want to tell them too soon, because it might scare them off, and they'll think I'm some sicko. But this was reality, and I needed to face my fear.

Ten years was long enough.

***

Knock, knock … Ding, dong.

I don't know how many times I've told my grandmother that she can just come in. She doesn't need to knock or ring the doorbell, she was welcomed anytime. I presumed she was just old-fashioned and didn't want to intrude.

Mary looked so vibrant the last few years. Instead of aging, I swear she looked younger—must be all that sleep she gets. It does wonders. "Drink lots of water and get plenty of sleep" was what she told people who wanted to know her secret. She was in her sixties but looked like she was in her forties. She must have found the fountain of youth. I would never say this to my mom, but they looked like they could be sisters. No joke.

"Good morning, Grandma," I said as I opened the door.

"Good morning, Trevor. By chance, can I steal a cup of coffee? My coffeemaker crapped out on me," Mary mumbled, sounding a little under the weather, as she pushed through the door like a zombie.

"I'll make a fresh pot for us, nice and strong," I replied as Mary followed me into the kitchen.

"Oh, Trevor. You are a lifesaver. By the way, how was your date with Amber? Did you finally meet her?"

"She cancelled on me again, but, at least this time, she came clean."

"Came clean about what?"

"The lies and why she was always so busy and why we couldn't meet. Come to find out, she was too nervous to show her face, since she pretended to be someone else."

"Why would someone do that? Eventually you would find out."

"Exactly. The worst part is she called me ignorant and superficial!"

"Seriously? She's the one pretending to be someone else for six months and wasting your time."

"I know. She's just insecure and upset that I didn't want to meet her anymore and ended the nonsense. She seemed nice and all, but it's kind of hard to start off a relationship with lies—hard to trust someone after that."

"I agree. You'll find someone, Trevor. Don't give up just because of one woman's ignorance."

"But what scares me the most, Grandma, is when do I divulge who Julia really is? Reality is that it could be a deal breaker," I said as I lowered my head in shame.

"That's really none of their business. You didn't know. No one knew. You have to let that go and forgive yourself, Trevor."

"Grandma, I can't hide from it like it never happened. Maybe facing my demons and truly forgiving myself is when I'll trust the person I decide to share my life with—a deep dark secret that could destroy me. Maybe that's the liberation I truly need to move on from this. That's why I've waited so long to date anyone. Fear of rejection and ridicule." I approached the cabinet and grabbed two coffee cups and poured the dark roast and handed one to Mary.

"Thank you, Trevor. Not to change the subject but I just wanted to bring something to your attention. When I went out to weed the garden yesterday, I noticed a dead bunny laying a few feet away. I dug a hole to bury it and thought maybe an animal had attacked it or it had gotten into a fight, but, when I picked it up, its neck had been broken."

"That's really strange. I wonder how that could've happened?"

Mary shrugged. "I'm not sure exactly, but maybe it climbed a tree, fell and broke its neck."

"But there are no trees near the garden. Can bunnies even climb trees?"

"They can climb a few feet when they feel they are in danger. Do you suppose an animal could've dragged it to the garden and left it there?"

"No clue. I guess it's possible. Anyway, I've been meaning to ask you, Grandma, if you've noticed anything different in Bella's behavior lately? Has she acted any differently around you?"

"The only thing I've noticed is she doesn't come by and visit as much as she used to, and, when she does, she seems much more quiet than normal. Is everything okay?"

"I'm not sure. I've tried talking to her, but she completely ignores me. She won't even acknowledge that I'm talking to her. When I took her to my parents' the night Amber and I were supposed to meet for our first date, she ran to her room, locked the door and refused to come out. I've also noticed she's been spending a lot more time in her treehouse lately. I think she's upset with me for dating—or at least trying to, since I never even got a chance to meet Amber in person after six months."

"I wouldn't worry too much about it. She'll grow out of it eventually. Probably just doesn't want another woman to take all your attention. Isabella adores you, Trevor. You know, that right?"

"I thought so, but now I'm starting to second guess myself. She has been so cold and distant the past few months. I don't know what to think anymore. I feel like I should just give up on the dating scene for a while and try to spend more time with Bella. I can feel her slipping away, and that's the last thing in this world I want to happen. I love her to pieces. She is my everything." I choked back tears as a hard lump formed in my throat.

"Trevor, you're an amazing father. You've devoted all your time and attention to Bella, and maybe that's why she's acting like a spoiled little brat right now. Sorry. Excuse my harsh words, but that's all I think it is. Isabella wants you all to herself. It's obvious she's a daddy's girl, and she's got you wrapped right around her little fingers. You can't let her control who you allow in your life, especially another female. I'm sure it'll hurt her feelings for a while, but she'll forgive you. I think having another woman in her life might be good, especially when she starts going through puberty. She might have a hard time talking to you about personal stuff like that. I'd hope she'd come to me or your mom, but she might think we're too old and don't understand what she's going through." Mary chuckled, trying to lighten the mood.

"You're right, Grandma. I shouldn't let Bella's behavior discourage me from dating. It's been a very lonely ten years. I desperately need another woman's touch. It's driving me crazy."

"I can only imagine, but please don't settle for the first woman you date because you're desperate. You have your whole life to find the right woman for you and Isabella."

"I won't, Grandma. I promise. Dating isn't all what it's cracked up to be. Hope I can find an honest one this time. I don't like being lied to or being played or any of the games. And I'll be damned if I find a money-hungry one."

"They call them gold diggers, Trevor. Get with the times. You're starting to sound like an old-timer." Mary chuckled. "You mean you don't want to be someone's sugar daddy?" Mary laughed.

"No way!"

"You have to be careful. The second they see your house, they'll drool. It'll be difficult to find someone who isn't after your money, 'cause all they'll see are dollar signs unless you can keep it at bay as long as you can. Make sure she's truly interested in you and not your money."

"I'll try, but it'll definitely be hard. They'll be curious why they can't come to my house and see how I live—probably think I'm hiding something, like I still live at home with Mommy and Daddy or embarrassed with how dirty my house is because I'm a bachelor and don't know how to clean."

"Let them think that. At least you know they like you and not your money."

"True."

"Oh, look at the time. I better get moving. I still have to jump in the shower and get ready. Going out for lunch with my friend, Annette. Thanks for the coffee, Trevor. I'll have to buy a new pot when I'm out."

"Thanks for stopping by, Grandma. It was nice talking with you. Don't be a stranger. You're welcome any time. I miss seeing you every day."

"Just trying to give you space."

"I don't need space, Grandma. I enjoy your company. You should come by later and have dinner with Bella and me. I'm making creamy Cajun chicken pasta."

"I wouldn't miss it for the world," Mary said with a wide grin as she closed the door behind her as she walked out.

Two Years Later

(Trevor)

Twilight had fallen. I stepped onto our back patio to enjoy the remarkable display of intense colors that painted the horizon with hues of magenta, tangerine, and lemon. A sliver of moon hovered alongside the few stars that now sprinkled the darkening sky. I loved nature and all the beauty beheld. I inhaled the scent of freshly cut grass and lilac trees, exhaled and melted into the chair as thoughts invaded my peaceful mind.

Two years had flown by so fast. I'd been on several dates with different women, but I finally met someone I really liked. Her name was Rachel. She was thirty-two and an investigative journalist for the *Redwood Times*, a local newspaper. She had long silky, strawberry-blond hair. She was tall and slender but boasted just enough curves in all the right places. And her emerald green eyes were mesmerizing. When Rachel looked at me, it was like I entered a hypnotic trance. But her looks were not what attracted me to her the most. It was her personality; she always seemed happy and tried to find the best in every situation, even the bad ones.

During our first lunch date, I had to skip out early. I had received a call from Bella's teacher, wanting to meet with me and saying it was urgent. Rachel had just smiled and said this gave us an excuse to meet up again soon, instead of getting upset with me.

A couple hours after I had to cut out early on our date, she texted and asked if everything was okay and was worried since the teacher had said it was urgent. She wasn't trying to pry to find out the details or anything, she just wanted to check on me. Having another woman care about me gave me butterflies.

We'd been exclusively dating for five months and four days—but who's counting? Best of all, she had no idea I have money and hadn't seen my house yet. She was understanding and liked how we took things slow and got to know each other. I can't wait for Bella to meet her. I think she'll really like Rachel; she's very sweet and kind.

I gazed in fascination at the brilliant starry night illuminating the heavens with thousands of stars, like diamond dust. The cool breeze rustled the leaves as the rhythmic percussion of endless waves disturbed the shimmering reflections in the lake. The crickets sang, and bats soared above, gliding in the most majestic way. Darkness cast a blanket of long shadows dancing through the endless night. The evening chill left behind a trail of goosebumps.

I grabbed some firewood from the stack in the corner, laid them in the firepit, drizzled lighter fluid over them, struck a match and threw it in. The flames leapt high and crackled as sparks flew toward the moon. The blanket of radiating warmth felt intoxicating. I could sit and stare in amazement for hours; fire had always been so mesmerizing to watch, twisting and curling in obscure shapes. This was the perfect night to relax under the radiant glow of the moon and twinkling stars while thinking of nothing but happy thoughts.

Life is good.

***

Rachel hated talking about the horrible events that surrounded her almost every day, plastering the papers and news channels. Even these terrible things would have some weight on even the happiest people. Learning to vent to those closest to her was something she needed some real work on. Rachel seemed happy on the outside, but I think she tried to hide a deep sadness, which inhibited her soul. A trait I could completely understand in her line of work. Rachel always said, for every negative, there is a positive, if you look deep enough and want to see the bright side of everything. She was an avid believer that everything happened for a reason. Her walls were camouflaged with wooden signs of quotes. *Eventually all the pieces fall into place. Until then, laugh at the confusion, live for the moment and know that everything happens for a reason.* And, *Trust that everything happens for a reason, even when you're not wise enough to see it.* Last but not least, *Don't lose hope. Everything happens for a reason. You never know what tomorrow may bring.* They made me believe that they were a daily reminder to keep her positive and thinking happy thoughts.

Tonight was the first time I sensed something really bothered Rachel. "Honey, is everything okay?"

"Yeah, of course," Rachel said softly as she pushed around her peas on her plate.

"You know, Rachel, you don't have to act like everything is fine and dandy all the time. You need to vent sometimes, and I'm the perfect person to take the beating. I can tell something is on your mind, and maybe you just need to get it off your chest."

"It's just this case. It's stumping everyone involved. Someone's vandalizing random places around town, and they have no leads. It's costing the business owners hundreds to thousands of dollars to repair. Windows smashed, the places trashed, lights broken, but they never take any money or steal any items. Usually someone breaks into a house because they're burglarizing it, but not a penny is taken nor is anything removed from the property, just vandalized. Why would someone do that?"

"I'm not sure. Maybe someone with some major anger issues? Maybe they pissed off a customer, and it's their way of getting back at them?"

"It's very random, and sweet, old people own most of the businesses, people who used their retirement money to invest into something they have a passion for, like books, artwork, travel agencies, fishing, and gift shops."

"Maybe they feel like the owners aren't a threat to them and won't press charges if they get caught? Who knows what goes on in the heads of some of these lunatics?"

Rachel forced a half smile. "I'm not going to dwell on it or let it ruin our night."

"Don't feel guilty for venting, Rachel. It's perfectly normal. I'm surprised you don't do it more often in your line of work. The news always seems to dwell on the negative. It's what hooks viewers into watching. No one cares about the good things. It's the drama that draws the most attention. It's so sad what society has become— depressed, stressed and anxiety-induced. I truly believe media has a lot to blame for this as well as the state of our culture. So sad to see everyone so addicted to social media, texting instead of talking or hanging out and spending time face to face. Society has become lazy and addicted to electronics instead of human interaction. It's quite depressing and only getting worse. Statistics show that three hundred and fifty million people worldwide suffer from depression." I sighed, hanging my head. "Do you know what I think?"

Rachel shook her head, leaning in closer.

"The internet needs to crash. We're so dependent on it. What did we do before computers?"

"We were much happier and more social," Rachel replied.

"Exactly. Don't get me wrong. The internet and computers are beneficial, but, since we're so reliant on them, our society would go into hysteria and panic and not know what to do with themselves."

"I totally agree with you, Trevor."

"Computers, videogames, and the internet have done extensive, irreputable harm to our society and culture. If we could only go back and fix the damage that has been done, this world would be a much happier place."

Rachel nodded. "It's just so sad, but true. I hate seeing everyone's faces stuck in their phones all the time. It's depressing. But enough of this depressive talk. Let's discuss something more enlightening and uplifting. Happy thoughts." Rachel forced a smile.

"You're right. Let's talk about you finally coming over to see my place. I think it's time, don't you?"

"Are you serious?"

"Absolutely!" I replied with an ear-to-ear grin.

ISABELLA
(BELLA)

Almost a year had transpired. After several school meetings with teachers, the principle, and the superintendent, my father decided the best option for me was to skip my seventh-grade year since it was quite apparent that I struggled in school due to boredom and needed to be challenged more. They all believed I was intellectually beyond kids my age. Teachers would call me *gifted*. I don't know if I generally liked that term to describe me.

I had to undergo a comprehensive psychological evaluation that measured intellectual functioning, academic skill levels, and social adjustment.

At first, I felt awkward being twelve years old in eighth grade. Everyone looked at me like I was some nerd. The friends I left a grade behind me stopped talking to me, saying I thought I was better than everyone else and that they were dumb. But skipping a grade had not been my decision; the decision had been made for me.

Yes, I felt bored in school, everything seemed too easy for me. It felt like what a third-grader would experience if they took kindergarten classes over again; it was that bad.

My eighth-grade peers showed me a complete opposite attitude. They looked down on me, like I was some young kid who couldn't compete at their intellectual level. But boy, did I prove them wrong. Any friends I did have, which wasn't many, wanted nothing to do with me anymore. They all thought I was a snob, which wasn't the case at all. I'm quiet and antisocial. I feel awkward in any social interactions. I just don't know what to say sometimes and can stand there speechless, like a complete idiot. Some would call me dumb, others called me a nerd, and even a troublemaker. They said teachers hadn't wanted to deal with me, so they made me skip a grade to get rid of me.

To be honest, skipping a grade did more harm than good. The once-quiet little girl had become more withdrawn and avoided conversations with even family members. School remained entirely too easy for me. I never had to study and always aced my tests and exams with no effort. I overheard kids saying they would spend hours after school completing their homework and studying, but it took me five minutes—no thought process involved, my hand would move faster than my mind. I found it quite strange that kids struggled so much in school when I found it entirely too easy.

I probably should have skipped more than just one grade, because even eighth grade proved too easy. Part of the extensive testing used to evaluate if skipping a grade was necessary defaulted to a schoolboard-approved IQ test. I received a score of 150, which was considered highly gifted.

***

I graduated high school at sixteen years old with an SAT score of 1600—the highest score possible. Too smart for my own good was what my family would say, especially

Dad. But boy was he proud of me. Which made me feel all warm and tingly inside.

Dad and I used to be really close, but after he started dating and I had skipped my seventh-grade year, I felt myself drifting from him. I don't think he understood what I endured emotionally. I wished my mom was here, so I could confide in her about these things, but she had died during childbirth. I felt alone not having a mom present. I'd heard all these stories in school, and it made me angry and jealous that they all had their moms, and I never even met mine. Dad and I discussed her, and I saw lots of pictures; I resembled her. Dad said I reminded him of her when he looked at me, which made me feel special, because, from the pictures I saw of my mom, she was a beautiful lady. I was tall and slender, with long honey-blond hair, big ice-blue eyes that complimented my long, thick eyelashes, high cheek bones, small nose, and full lips.

I truly believed things would have turned out differently if my mom had been around when I was growing up. I would lay in bed during sleepless nights and talk out loud to my mom, telling her everything that happened in my life—what bothered me, what kids said at school about me, how I felt so alone and felt like I couldn't talk to anyone about it except her. I asked her what I should do or how she felt about everything, like she could hear me from the heavens, but she never responded. Who was I kidding? She was dead; she can't talk, and she sure can't hear me. She's laying six feet underground, rotting in a coffin for the last sixteen years.

***

Tonight was the night, July 27. The super-blue-blood moon—a once-in-a-lifetime rare occurrence when a blue moon, super moon, blood moon, and lunar eclipse occur concurrently while the moon is at its closest point to Earth—presented the longest total-lunar eclipse of the twenty-first century, lasting for an entire hour and forty-three minutes. I was super excited to experience this anomaly with my own eyes but also frustrated the news twisted this amazing phenomenon into Breaking News, reporting a "prophecy alert." It was the longest blood moon ever, and the media claimed it as an "apocalyptic sign of the end of the world," which the Bible referenced.

I've always had an intense passion for space and the unknown—the sun, moon, stars, and planets. When I turn eighteen, I want to get a tattoo on my left shoulder blade of a half-moon/half-sun with the north, east, south, and west rays intertwined. The illustration I had drawn was captivating. I loved to draw and read. They were how I escaped from my desolate, exacerbated life and forgot about everything and everyone around me. I had a habit of reading until my eyes go cross-eyed. Books had a grotesque effect on my vise-grip mind by distorting reality in an unexpected ludicrous demeanor. My ultimate escape from reality. It was so addicting and intoxicating. It gave me a feeling of euphoria; I just couldn't get enough. I could totally lose myself; it was the only time I felt enraptured and at peace.

I stepped outside as the refreshing night breeze gently caressed my delicate skin. I noticed a leaf directly above me, slowly drifting and swaying like a pendulate. A gust lifted it and tossed it like a ragdoll into the blanket of darkness etched in charcoal.

Dad sat in his chair, holding a cold beer and gazing at the sky. He smiled when he saw me. "Hi, sweetie. Have you come to join me for the show?"

"I wouldn't miss it for the world!"

Dad pointed. "Look!"

Thousands of fireflies in our backyard glowed dim then intensified in magnitude. I'd never seen so many fireflies in my life. I stared in awe as my backyard resembled thousands of twinkling stars just in an arm's reach, as if the fireflies had come to enjoy the total-lunar eclipse from our spectacular view.

The super-blue-blood moon glowed with brilliance as its reflection rippled in the lake, casting a red tint in the sparkling water of diamonds. This beautiful moment would be etched in my memory forever and never forgotten.

COLLEGE
(BELLA)

Starting school at Hollins University in Roanoke terrified me. I didn't know a soul, but not like that mattered much anyways, since I didn't have any friends. I had a full scholarship. I didn't want to attend a school too far from home but wanted one to be far enough away where I could have some privacy. Being only a little over an hour away, I could technically still live at home, but I wanted some independence, even as much as it frightened me. I was the youngest student on campus. Sixteen and in college—it's hard to wrap my head around.

My roommate, Carrie Evans, was nineteen and in her second year—a redhead with long wavy hair, emerald-green eyes, and lightly freckled skin. I learned quickly that she loved to get drunk, go to parties, and have fun. She was popular and had lots of friends. I wasn't sure in the beginning if we would get along, being so different on every aspect in life, but we became the best of friends. She got me to open up more and be more social, but it still made me uncomfortable. I didn't like drinking too much either. I got so drunk at my first frat party that I passed out and didn't remember what had happened the next day. My head pounded all day, and I felt nauseated. I guess I vomited everything I had drank that night but don't remember any of it. Having a hangover sucks.

"Promise me that you'll never let me drink that much again, Carrie."

"Why would I promise you that? You had lots of fun last night! There's another party tonight. We should go."

"I don't know, Carrie. I feel like I was hit by a freight train. I don't think I'll recover by this evening. The last thing on my mind right now is having another drink."

"You're a lightweight. Just hang out with me, and you'll be a pro at drinking." Carrie laughed. "I'll even teach you all the tricks to not have a hangover the next morning."

"Would've been nice if you told me some of those tricks last night."

"I didn't realize you drank too much, until it was too late."

"I don't feel very good." I grabbed my stomach and ran to the bathroom. I lifted the toilet seat and violently vomited as my stomach convulsed. "I think I'm still drunk. The room is spinning," I yelled from the bathroom as I wiped my mouth with the back of my hand. "I think I'm going to lay down for a bit. Maybe when I wake up, I'll feel better." I dragged my feet as I shambled to my bed and plopped face first into the pillow.

"Okay, Bella. I'm going to meet Chad for lunch. When I come back, I'll wake you."

"Sounds good. Have fun," I replied, my voice muffled from talking through the pillow.

***

"Bella. Bella. Wake up. Bella. Wake up," Carrie whispered as she shook me.

"I'm awake. I'm awake. What's wrong, Carrie?"

"I screwed up! I don't know what to do. I don't trust anyone else. They all have big mouths, and Chad would eventually find out. Can I trust you to keep a secret, Bella?"

"Yeah, of course, Carrie. What is it? What happened?" I rubbed my eyes and sat upright in bed as Carrie sat next to me, buried her head in her hands and sobbed. I rubbed her back, trying to comfort her.

She took a moment to gather herself, then she straightened up as black mascara streaked her wet cheeks. "I'm pregnant," Carrie choked out as she nervously rotated her engagement ring on her finger.

"Why are you so upset? Don't you want to have a baby with Chad? You've been together since high school."

"I know. I do. But I don't think it's Chad's. I've cheated on him a few times with this guy named Ryan. I've been meeting up with him behind Chad's back. I feel so guilty now, but, at the time, it was fun and exhilarating. He's exciting, confident, and very good looking. He makes my heart skip a beat. But I've been with Chad since freshman year. He's my high-school sweetheart. He proposed to me when we graduated. We've been together for six years, engaged for two of them. I love Chad, I really do, but I second-guessed myself about whether I'd made the right decision—we *have been* dating since I was *fourteen*. He's the only boyfriend I've ever had. I've never been with anyone else except for Ryan. I don't know what to do, Bella."

"I don't think you should leave Chad because you found some new exciting guy. Do you know anything about this guy except that you think he's hot and a good lay?"

"Not really. He's the quarterback for Virginia Tech. His best friend Jason attends school here, so he's been to a couple frat parties. That's how I met him."

"Let me give you some advice, Carrie. Don't leave Chad. He's your high-school sweetheart. You're engaged. You love him. Ryan is just a fling. He's probably sleeping with lots of other girls too. He's the quarterback for Virginia Tech—come on now, you can't think he'll stay faithful to you. Besides, we live forty-five minutes away. Don't screw things up with Chad. This guy might be a complete asshole and just trying to be charming to get into your pants. If you tell Ryan that you're pregnant, he might laugh and leave you high and dry 'cause he won't want to deal with some pregnant girl he doesn't even know and only slept with a few times. You might be raising the baby all alone without a father. You know if you told Chad, he would step up to the plate. I won't tell a soul. You have my word. Just promise you'll stop seeing this Ryan guy and stay faithful to Chad. He really loves you, Carrie. I can tell by the way he looks at you. I hope someday a guy will look at me the way Chad looks at you."

"I know, Bella. You're right. Chad is an amazing boyfriend. He treats me like a princess. I don't know what I was thinking. I'll stop seeing Ryan and tell Chad I'm pregnant. Thanks for talking some sense into me, Bella. You're really something special. Want to be the baby's godmother?"

"I would love to. I feel honored," I replied with a huge grin as I wrapped my arms around Carrie and gave her a big hug.

E. A. Owen

BEST FRIENDS
(BELLA)

After I swore to keep Carrie's little dirty secret, we became best friends. She confided in me with just about everything, and I reciprocated. Our friendship was unorthodox, outrageous and exciting.

"Who was your best friend growing up, Bella?" Carrie asked as she took a big bite of her burger.

"I never really had any close friends. I've always been quiet and kept to myself. The only person I ever considered a friend was my neighbor, Lindsey. She used to come over and play in my treehouse that my dad and grandfather built for me. But once I skipped seventh grade, she wanted nothing to do with me anymore. I don't know what got into her, but she became a real bully. Even when I minded my own business, she would seek me out. Once, when I sat next to her in the cafeteria, she shot me this snotty look, grabbed her tray and sat at a table across the room. Everyone else looked at me, rolled their eyes and sat at the table with Lindsey, leaving me by myself at an empty table in a crowded cafeteria. I ate in silence, trying to hold back the tears that trickled down my cheeks. I stood and walked with my head down, and, as I passed Lindsey's table, she stuck out her foot and tripped me. It caught me off guard, and I fell. My tray slipped from my grip and hit a kid in the back of the head. In anger, he got up, spun around and smashed his fist into my face. I felt warm blood dribble from my nose and splatter on the floor. Everyone pointed their fingers and laughed. I burst into tears and ran out of the cafeteria. I heard people mocking me and calling me a crybaby. I've never been so humiliated in my life. That was just the beginning. Lindsey got worse. Sometimes I'd walk into the classroom and she'd turn to her friends and bark, saying, 'Look, the dog just walked in.' Everyone would laugh uncontrollably. I grew to hate Lindsey. She became my nemesis. But the bullying eventually stopped. A few months later, a devastating fire took her entire family, and they all died in their sleep."

"Oh, my God, Bella. That's awful! How did you handle the news?"

"At first, I was shocked and devastated. I couldn't believe her entire family was dead. But, at the same time, I was relieved the bullying would stop. I know that sounds horrible to say, but, Carrie, it got so bad that I didn't even want to live anymore. I became extremely depressed. I cut myself to cope with the intense emotions I felt. I skipped school and cried myself to sleep almost every night. The only thing that seemed to relieve the pain was to cut myself—the deeper, the better. Once I cut so deep that I'm sure I needed stitches, but I couldn't tell my dad, so I used superglue. It stopped the bleeding in a pinch and sealed the wound, with less scarring. It worked pretty good. See?" I lifted my shirt to expose the faded scar on my left side. "She

E. A. Owen

was just unscrupulous and deviant. It's like she was possessed. We used to get along, then it seemed like something in her snapped, and she hated me and just looked for ways to make my life miserable." My internal temperature rose; I got angry just thinking about it. "I tried to put it all behind me, forget it had ever happened. I don't like talking about it, makes me get all crazy, remembering the Hell she'd put me through. I guess she got what she deserved!" I inhaled quickly and held my breath after I realized I had just said that out loud. "I should have never said that. I just got carried away, reliving the nightmare she had put me through. I didn't mean it. I'm sorry, Carrie. I was upset. Can we talk about something else?"

"Don't get upset with yourself, Bella. It's completely understandable. I can't imagine what she put you through. I'm sure anyone in your situation would feel relieved or had wished her dead at one point or another. It's not like you killed her. No need to apologize to me. Have you ever talked to anyone about what she put you through? The emotions you felt? The cutting? Like a counselor or maybe a teacher, your dad, your grandmother? Anyone?"

"No. You're the only other person I've talked to about this besides my great-grandmother. Not even my dad knows."

"Well, you have to start somewhere. It's a good first step. Venting can help, but you might consider talking to a professional, and maybe they'll help you heal those wounds that are still wide open and let you feel confident in putting this all behind you. I'm so sorry, Bella. I can't imagine what you went through. I'm here for you whenever you need to talk. But I think you're right. Let's talk about something different." Carrie smiled as she reached in for a big hug.

There was a long pause before I broke the silence. "Have you decided what you want to major in, Carrie?"

"I'm considering working in a field within the FBI. I'm not sure exactly what yet. So, in the time being, I'm taking criminal justice classes. How about you?"

"I want to be a dentist or a veterinarian. Haven't decided yet." I paused. "Do you think your baby will complicate your schooling? Do you plan on taking a break from school?"

"I haven't thought that far ahead. I hope I can finish school. It just might take a little longer to get my degree though. I may have to go to school part time for a year."

"Makes sense." I paused. "Have you and Chad discussed when you'll get married?"

"I actually wanted to talk to you about that. Chad and I think it's best if we get married before the baby is born, and I was hoping you'd be my maid of honor."

"Are you serious?" I replied with pure excitement.

"Absolutely! You're my best friend."

"I would love to, Carrie. I feel so honored you thought of me." I gave Carrie a big hug, squeezing tight.

"We only have a month to prepare everything for the wedding, so we better get cracking."

MURDER

(TREVOR)

Eight Years Later

I quickly glanced behind me, breathing heavy and running as fast as my legs could carry me. Trying to catch my balance, I tripped several times on twisted overgrown roots that protruded from the forest ground. Sharp rocks and dry leaves tore up my bare feet, leaving a trail of scented warm blood behind me. My heart pounded so hard that I could hear it throbbing inside my skull. I had to stop and take a break for just a moment to catch my breath. My throat felt dry and scratchy from gasping desperately for air. I frantically search every direction—eyes wide with fear.

The darkness played tricks on me. I noticed a shadow dart behind a nearby tree. I gasped, holding my breath and hoping not to be heard by whoever or whatever chased me. The echo of snapping sticks startled me as I fought the impulse to turn around. My heart pounded fiercely; my fingers curled into a fist, nails digging into my palms. Fear tortured my thoughts as my stomach slowly twisted into a tense cramp.

A drop of water hit the top of my head. I tossed back my head, noticing streaks of moonlight dancing through the treetops as the wind rustled the leaves. A loud crash paralyzed my soul as I released a curdling scream.

***

I awoke from a sound sleep, drenched in a fear-induced sweat. I must have really been out cold. I can't remember the last time I dreamt so vividly. I wiped sweat off my trembling body. *Gross.*

A cool breeze invaded my room as the curtains swayed from side to side. I glanced at the alarm clock on my nightstand—3:28 a.m. A bolt of lightning ripped violently through the once-silent night followed by a loud clap of thunder, startling me and making me feel like I had literally jumped out of my skin

I threw the blankets off me and leapt from bed. The wind howled as rain blew right through my open window, dripping on the hardwood floors. I almost fell, slipping in a puddle that had formed under my window. I loved thunderstorms, but the enjoyment stopped when it decided to creep indoors. I slammed shut the window and glanced at the dark sky illuminated with explosions of static lightning.

What was I running from? I was truly terrified! The dream felt so real.

I sat on the side of my bed and gazed through the window of distorted images as I drifted back to sleep.

***

I've had the same recurring dream for the last ten years. It doesn't always happen the same way or at the same location, but I'm always running from something, induced by fear and woken up abruptly before I ever see who or what I was running from. I've researched the meaning of the dream online and in a dream dictionary I kept in my office. It worried me so much that I even saw a therapist.

I was concerned my subconscious was trying to warn me of something, but, of what, I'm not exactly sure. Some references say it's stress or anxiety, others say it could represent running away from the truth. It could be a feeling of being trapped in the daily grind of life and wanting to escape. Also, it might represent me avoiding an issue or a person. But they all said the same thing—what chases you matters. Problem was that I never see who or what chases me in any of the dreams, so I feel lost.

I've probably had the dream a hundred times in the last ten years. It definitely creeps me out.

***

"Honey, could you not sleep again last night?" I asked as I approached the half-empty coffeepot to pour myself a cup.

"I slept okay until about three then just tossed and turned. I didn't want to wake you, so I came out here," Rachel said as she covered her mouth and yawned. "I should have never turned on the TV. I just can't escape this nightmare. It's everywhere I turn—at work, on the radio and TV, in the newspaper. No one knows how to have a normal conversation anymore. All they do is talk about it. The entire town is obsessed. I get it. Nothing like this has ever happened around here before. This used to be a safe town. People would leave their cars and homes unlocked. They were happy, or at least appeared to be. But now everyone looks over their shoulders, locks their doors, and doesn't go out as much. And when they do, it's all they think about and talk about. It's making me sick to my stomach. I just want to get away from here for a while and try to enjoy ourselves. Maybe go on vacation …"

I noticed the bags under Rachel's eyes have worsened. "Let's do it then. I'll take the time off from work. We can go anywhere you want, baby." I sat next to her on the couch and put my hand on her knee.

"I don't know if my boss will let me have any time off, Trevor. I desperately need a vacation, but work is so crazy right now. Everyone is working around the clock. I probably won't be able to leave until the killer is behind bars and the town feels safe again. The murder happened too close to home." Rachel slouched her shoulders and sighed.

"It's okay, sweetheart. We'll go whenever we get a chance." I tried to force a smile as I took a sip of my much-needed coffee.

"Have you talked to Isabella lately? See how she's handling the news and see what she's doing for extra precautions to keep herself safe from this maniac roaming the streets?"

"I tried calling her a couple times. But she's so busy with work, she hasn't called me back yet. Maybe I'll stop into her office today and surprise her, see if she can take a lunch break and grab a bite with me."

"I'm sure she'd really like that." Rachel leaned in for a kiss. "I should go. Gus wants to have a staff meeting this morning. I've got to stop and pick up rolls on my way into work."

"Okay, honey. Have a good day. I'll see you later tonight. I love you."

"I love you too, babe," Rachel said as she closed the door behind her.

I haven't seen Mary in a couple days. I wonder what she's been up to.

I refilled my coffee cup and walked to the guest house. *Knock, knock.*

I waited a few moments—no answer.

KNOCK, KNOCK, KNOCK!

That's weird. Mary is always up bright and early.

I headed to the attached garage and glanced in the window. Her car was parked inside.

Maybe she stayed up late last night and is just sleeping in. I'll swing by after work and see how she's doing.

The drive to work seemed longer than normal, probably since I'm riding in complete silence. I turned on the radio, but every station plastered the airwaves with news of the murder that had happened a few weeks ago. Rachel's right—the media just took this to a whole new level, acting like nothing else in the world was happening right now. I got sick of hearing about it.

A long wailing scream pierced my silent drive. I pulled to the roadside to let the police cruisers zip past. I counted six of them.

Must be something serious.

I shrugged. I'm sure I'll hear all about it when I get home tonight. Rachel knew everything about everything. Rachel *was* the news. As much as she acted like she hated her job, I secretly thought she enjoyed all the drama. It added a little spice to her boring life.

***

I made it to Bella's office just in time to catch her before she walked out the door.

"Bella, you free to grab lunch with your old man? My treat. We can head to the bistro you enjoy so much and see what the special is today."

"Sure, Dad. Sorry I never returned your calls. I've been super busy lately. I'm running a special right now, and we're getting an overwhelming response."

"That's fantastic, honey. What special is that?"

"We're offering cleanings for new clients for just forty-eight bucks. It's just a basic cleaning, nothing extravagant. But you would never believe how many people don't see a dentist on a regular basis. Some of them haven't had a cleaning for five to fifteen years. I'm booked for the next six months straight. It's just been insane!"

"I'm so proud of you, Isabella."

"Thanks, Dad. Business is better than I ever imagined. By the way, how are you and Rachel doing?"

"Good. She's been busy with the killer on the loose. How are you dealing with the drama and news?"

"I guess I haven't really had a chance to let it soak in at all. I've just been balls to the wall with appointments. But at least it keeps me out of trouble." Isabella chuckled. "I'm so glad you came by and asked me to lunch, Dad. It's so nice to see you. It seems like it's been such a long time."

"We miss seeing you, Isabella. I'm sure Mary misses you too. I haven't seen her in a couple days. I stopped by her place and knocked on the door before I left for work this morning, but she never answered. She must be sleeping in."

"*Hmmm*, that's odd. She loves sitting on the front porch with her coffee first thing in the morning, watching the sunrise. She says her day starts off on the wrong foot if she wakes up late and misses it. You know, Dad? She's getting old. You should keep a closer eye on her and check up on her more often. She's in her eighties."

"I know. But you must admit, she gets around great for her age. She goes out and plays Bingo every Tuesday and Thursday night, has friends over to her place and plays cards and cribbage. She goes antique shopping, travels and stays busy for her old age, but it keeps her healthy." I paused. "I'm sure she would love to show you her old stomping ground back in South Dakota. You should plan a trip with her sometime before she, um, you know, gets too old and can't do much anymore."

"I would love to, Dad, but I've been so busy lately—with school, then finding work, now starting my own dental practice. I don't have time to take a vacation."

"I'm sure you can figure out something. Mary won't be around forever, and you'll kick yourself if you never took a trip with her before she passes."

"You're right. I'll look into it, Dad. I promise."

***

It happened again. Another murder. This was two now, just six weeks apart. The town freaked out. We thought it was bad before, but now it's complete chaos. People threatened to move. They don't feel safe here anymore, wondering when the next one will happen and where. First one happened in Roanoke, the second in Salem, just ten miles away.

The media had not released the details of the murders yet, which I thought was best since the town had already come unglued. Their sanity fell to pieces and were scattered amongst the perplexed turbulence of chaos. The nightmare had just gotten worse with a second murder. It was not just the one anymore, and, if another happened, we'd have a serial killer on our hands. To be honest, it was scary on so many levels, because it happened to us, which made it real.

Serial killers had always fascinated me. I wasn't a psycho or anything. I just never understood how another human being could be so methodical and purposely take another's life. So much evil existed in this world. I had always found psychology and the human mind very intriguing. I should have majored in psychology instead of engineering—much more interesting. I considered it at one point in college but talked myself out of it. I thought that line of work would be too depressing, listening to people's problems all the time.

The scariest part was that the killer could be anyone— my next-door neighbor, a coworker, someone standing next to me in line at Starbuck's or sitting by me at a restaurant. It was enough to make anyone insane. Jeez, it could be the pizza delivery guy, the mailman, the bank teller, or the cashier at the grocery store. It could literally be anyone. Paranoia, at its best.

Since discovering that my great-great grandfather is Aaron Kosminiski, aka Jack the Ripper, I've wondered how differently my life may have been if I was not related to a serial killer, especially one never punished for his crimes. A London witch had put a curse on our family, but I'm sure karma had a role as well. I was naturally curious, so I took a psychology class in college before I decided against majoring in psychology. It was very interesting, to say the least. I clearly remembered a class discussion about our opinion surrounding systematic manipulation—an assumption that an event affects behavior. Were killers born or were they made? My honest opinion was that killers were made, but some studies have shown that psychopathy is 60% inherited.

What summarized the main traits of a psychopath? A disturbed, callous individual with blunted emotions, impulsive tendencies incapable of feeling guilt or remorse. Psychopaths don't feel nervous or embarrassed when caught doing something bad. They don't feel sad when others suffer. Even though they feel physical pain, they do not suffer from emotional pain. They feel no empathy or guilt. They are pure evil.

Some creepy, twisted quotes from serial killers reveal the darkest parts of the human psyche:

"I don't feel guilt for anything. I feel sorry for people who feel guilt." Ted Bundy

"It wasn't as dark and scary as it sounds. I had a lot of fun ... killing somebody's a funny experience." Albert DeSalvo.

"I actually think I may be possessed with demons." Dennis Rader

"I killed them as cold as ice, and I would do it again, and I know I would kill another person, because I've hated humans for a long time." Aileen Wuornos

"We've all got the power in our hands to kill, but most people are afraid to use it. The ones who aren't afraid, control life itself ... Even psychopaths have emotions, then again, maybe not." Richard Ramirez.

"You got to realize, you're the Devil as much as you're God." Charles Manson. He also once said that his only regret was that he did not kill more people.

One of the scariest parts about serial killers was how well they blended with the rest of society. We'd never know if a psychopath or murderer sat right next to us.

SOUTH DAKOTA
(BELLA)

Knock, Knock, Knock.

I was getting impatient. I have no idea what Great-grandma Mary would say. The sun beat down like molten lava, filling the sky with its brilliance and a radiant glow that cast shadows.

I wish she would hurry up. There I go again, unannounced and expecting the world to just snap its fingers at my beck and call. At least I recognized when I was being ridiculous. I rolled my eyes at the thoughts that infringed my fragile mind.

Footsteps approached the door. "Isabella, what do I have the honor to see you on this fine morning?"

"Great-grandma, pack your bags. I'm taking you to South Dakota."

Mary looked taken aback by the surprise. She donned a blank stare then smiled, turning and walking away.

"Do you need me to help you grab anything?"

I noticed dirty dishes in the sink and on the counters, mail scattered on the table, and a stench of rotten food that left my stomach unsettled. This was not like Mary at all. She had always been a clean freak since I could remember—nothing out of place, very orderly and spotless. Her house always smelled so nice too. The air captured the sweet, savory aromas of freshly baked pies, cookies, and fresh ground coffee—a blend of perfection, like walking into a bakery. But now the smell was almost repulsive. How could she live like this?

"Is everything okay, Great-grandma? Dad says he hasn't seen you much lately. Do you still get up every morning and watch the sunrise?"

"I haven't in a while. I've been so tired that I don't know what's wrong with me lately." Mary stumbled around her room, aimlessly looking for something.

"Can I help you find something?"

Mary stood there a while, looking at the ceiling.

"Are you feeling okay? Do you need to sit down?"

"I'm fine, Natalie. Just give me a minute."

"Who's Natalie?" I asked, confused.

"Oh, my. Did I call you *Natalie*? I meant Isabella. I'm sorry, sweetie."

"I took the week off from work, so we could spend some time together. I've been so busy lately that I haven't had a chance to come visit you in a while. Thought you could show me the town in South Dakota where you grew up. I've never been. I've heard the Midwest is a quiet, peaceful place. I need that kind of break right now from my chaotic life. Just take a breather and spend some quality time with you, if that's okay?"

"I'd love to, Natalie. Just let me grab my things, and we can be on our way."

Natalie? Why does she keep calling me Natalie?

I left the room and texted Dad. *Who is Natalie? Great-grandma keeps calling me* Natalie.

I paced back and forth, waiting for Dad's response. Mary wasn't being much of a help letting me know what I could do to help. I scanned the filthy room and tidied it. Just as I finished, my phone buzzed in my pocket. I wiped my hands on a nearby towel and read the reply from Dad. *Natalie was her daughter. My mother.*

I called Dad's phone, thinking texting would take too long.

"Hello?"

"Hey, Dad. I don't think Great-grandma is doing so well. She wanders around like she's a lost puppy, calling me *Natalie*. Maybe this trip wasn't such a good idea. She doesn't even know who I am. Do you think she might have Alzheimer's, like Great-aunt Angel?"

"It's possible. It can be genetic. Besides, Mary is in her eighties. Just go and try to have a good time. Don't let Mary out of your sight. Have a safe trip. Let me know when you get there. Love you."

"Love you too, Dad. Bye."

***

We had a two-hour layover in Chicago, and my eyes already grew tired. I couldn't let myself drift off to sleep. Mary might wander off and get lost, and I'd never find her. She didn't even own a cell phone. She's old fashion that way, but what could I really expect? She was in her eighties, for Heaven's sake.

I sat back to observe Mary interact with other people since she worried me with her unusual behavior. I noticed she would talk to someone, and, in mid-sentence, pause, look around aimlessly then just wander off, leaving the other person puzzled and confused. I thought Mary must forget what she was talking about, gets embarrassed and walks away. I can't imagine what she goes through, living in a mind with faded memories that's broken into thousands of pieces unable to be reassembled, lost in a world of confusion.

I hoped I won't get Alzheimer's. It worried me sometimes, especially when I'd run back in the house several times before leaving for the day because I kept forgetting something, or I'd enter a room and forget why I went in there. Not a good sign at such an early age.

The scariest part would be to forget loved ones, to not even know who they were—just another stranger amongst the millions. One of my favorite books was *The Notebook* by Nicholas Sparks. I hoped someday I found a man who would love me that much. Even though she had no clue he was her husband, he visited her every day and read to her, to remind her of everything she had forgotten, in hopes of regaining her memory. It was the ultimate love story and a real tearjerker.

Another real scare would be to completely lose myself, like Mary had started to do—not waking up early to watch the sunrise, something she said she would never miss, because it held so much beauty and promise. She always said it started off her day on the right track. Her house was always clean and orderly and smelled amazing, which now was a complete pigsty and smelled of rotten food.

I doubted Mary would be much of a tour guide when we arrive to her hometown. Had she forgotten the house where she grew up or the house she had spent forty years before she moved to Virginia to be close to us?

A loud announcement blared over the intercom, informing passengers that our flight to Minneapolis now boarded. At least our final layover in Minneapolis, Minnesota to Sioux Falls, South Dakota was only forty-five minutes.

I scanned the crowds of people but could not find Mary. I panicked. I had seen her just a moment ago, but I had gotten lost in thought and stopped watching her. I rushed to the bathroom, thinking maybe she had to use the restroom, but just a woman and her child were in there. I ran down the long corridor, looking in every direction, wide-eyed with fear. I can't believe I lost her. Dad had even warned me to keep close watch of her. I didn't even care if we missed our flight; we could catch another one later. I needed to find Mary.

Where could she have wandered off to? Maybe she got hungry or thirsty and strolled to a nearby café. I checked Tortas Frontera, Carry-Out Carry-On, Burrito Beach, and Rush Street; she was nowhere to be found. I felt like I was suffocating, and the walls were closing in on me.

I had to think quick. This airport was gigantic; she could be anywhere. She could have left the airport or tried boarding another plane. Maybe she was boarding our plane, and I wasn't there because I was running around, looking for her. The thoughts infesting my mind made my head spin. My stomach twisted in knots as I ran.

I caught a glimpse in the corner of my eye and slowed down. Mary sat alone, gazing at the television.

I plopped into a chair next to her. "Great-grandma, our plane started boarding. If we want to make the flight, we better get over there quickly or they'll leave without us."

Mary stared with fright in her eyes. "Can you believe there's a killer loose in Virginia? He's killed two people. What is this world coming to, Natalie? These are the reasons I don't own a television set. The news is so negative and depressing. The media always seems to focus on all the bad stuff."

"Great-grandma, we've got to go. Let me help you up. We can talk more about this on the plane."

We didn't make it back in time. The gate was closed. I glanced out the window and watched as our plane taxied down the runway.

I sighed heavily. *At least I found Mary. That's all that matters.*

Planes had always given me major anxiety. I'd always had a gut-wrenching feeling every time the plane takes off, like something bad would happen. I had a terrible dream the day after I had booked our flight. The plane engine had issues in midflight, and it caught on fire. Flames blazed red hot and wild. The fear felt too real. The plane hurtled downward at tremendous speeds, similar to the feeling when a roller coaster plummets at full speed and I can't scream, my throat dropping to the pit of my stomach and I can't catch my breath. I loved the thrill and excitement, but, at the same time, I hated it, always afraid something would go wrong, like the wheels would leave the track and we'd all crash down. It's a weird love/hate thing. I can't get enough of the thrill; it's intoxicating but scary.

Later that night in the hotel, after Mary had fallen asleep, I flipped on the news.

Breaking News: Flight 458 from Chicago to Minneapolis crashed, leaving no survivors. The cause for the crash is under investigation.

My eyes widened with fear as dread fell upon me like a crashing wave.

We were supposed to be on that flight!

BAD LUCK
(BELLA)

"Just lovely!" I slammed my fists against the steering wheel. "What else is going to go wrong on this trip?"

I opened the rental car's driver side door and walked to the passenger side. I kicked the flat tire in frustration. I paced back and forth, cussing and shaking my fists in the air.

"Just great! Great-grandma, can you pop the trunk?" I yelled from the rear of the car.

The trunk popped open, and I searched the spare tire well, but it was empty. "No spare? Are you kidding me!"

I slammed the trunk and grabbed my cellphone from the car. "I called roadside assistance. They said they would get a driver here in an hour. I saw a gas station a mile back if you're hungry. You think you could walk two miles?"

Mary chuckled. "I may be old, but I'm not disabled. I do have two legs, sweetheart."

"Or we can just sit here and wait. It's up to you."

"We've been doing a lot of sitting. Let's stretch our legs. I could use a coffee."

Twenty minutes later, we arrived at Casey's General Store. I ordered a sandwich, and Mary made a coffee.

"This sandwich, and she has a small coffee." I pointed to Mary sitting at a nearby table. I handed the store keeper my card.

"I apologize, but our internet is down." A short plump lady with streaks of gray hair and a small button-nose pointed to a sign next to the register. "We can only accept cash and local checks at this time."

I fumbled through my purse, looking for change, but all I had was a couple quarters, a dime, and three pennies— clearly not enough to cover my sandwich and Mary's coffee. "We're from Virginia. We flew in last night. Our rental got a flat tire about a mile away. We walked here, since roadside assistance said they couldn't come for an hour. I'm sorry, but all I have is my card. Will this at least cover the coffee?" I held out all the change I had in my hand.

"Your sandwich and coffee are on the house," the lady said with a big grin.

"Are you sure?"

"Of course. Sounds like you ladies are having a rough day."

"Thank you, ma'am. You're very kind," I replied with a smile.

"Where are you ladies headed to?"

"Astoria."

"I've heard of the town, just not sure exactly where it's at."

"My great-grandma lived there almost her entire life. She moved to Virginia to be close to us when I was just five years old. Astoria has a population of about sixty people. I think it's by a town called Toronto."

"Oh yeah. I've heard of Toronto. They have a diner known for their good food. I've been meaning to get up there one of these days and try it out, just haven't made it yet. I believe it's called Toronto Café."

"Nice to know. I'll have to try it out while we're here. Thanks for the sandwich and coffee. We really appreciate it."

"Yeah, no problem at all. Hope your day gets better."

I smiled. "Thanks."

"Great-grandma, we better get back to the car before the tow truck shows up and we're not there."

"I can give you a ride," the storekeeper hollered.

"Are you sure?"

"Yeah, no problem at all. I'll just lock the front door and hang the Closed sign. No one will probably show up in the short five minutes I'm gone anyways."

"Thank you!"

"I never caught your name. My name is Julie." Julie extended her hand.

"Hi, Julie. My name is Isabella, but most people just call me Bella." I gently shook her hand.

"Well, Bella, it's nice to meet you. Have a safe rest of your trip."

"Thanks, Julie, for the coffee, sandwich, and ride."

"No problem at all. Glad I could help," Julie said with a smile.

We reached the car just in time. The tow truck pulled behind the rental when Julie let us out of the car. In no time flat, the mechanic fixed the tire, and we were on our way. No pun intended.

***

"Seriously, what the hell is going on now?" I asked through gritted teeth.

The car's engine sputtered and stopped. I had just enough time to coast to the shoulder before it completely died.

"Just lovely!" I yelled.

I looked at the gages, and the gas tank read Empty. How did I not notice? I guess I had just assumed when we left the rental place that it had a full tank of gas. I figured we had enough to get us to Astoria but apparently not. I grabbed my phone, but I had no service. I exited the vehicle and walked with my phone held above my head, trying to find a signal. Nothing.

"You won't get any service out here. It's a dead zone," Mary said as she hung out the passenger window.

"What are we going to do?"

"If you walk a little farther, you might pick up a bar or two. Just don't know how far you have to walk. You might get lucky."

"This trip has been nothing but unlucky!" I snapped and immediately felt bad. Mary hadn't done anything wrong; this wasn't her fault. I sighed heavily. "I'll be back."

I walked for ten minutes before I got a bar and could place a phone call. But, just as someone answered the other end, the call dropped.

"Dammit!" I kicked a rock into the ditch.

I spun around and heard a car approaching; although I couldn't see it yet. Maybe if I flag them down, they could somehow help us.

The car came into view, and I waved my arms. The car slowed and pulled over.

"Do you know where the closest gas station is?" I asked.

"Yeah, about six miles east of here. Do you need a ride?" a man asked, with a full gray beard, long hair, and wearing torn and dirty clothes.

"My car ran out of gas, and I don't have any service."

The man smiled, showing a mouth full of missing teeth. "Hop in. I'll give you a ride."

"My great-grandma is waiting in the car."

"She can come with." He spat on the ground outside his window, just barely missing my shoe. "You're not from around here, are you?"

"No, sir. Just came to visit my great-grandma's hometown."

"I'm picking up a southern accent."

"We're from Virginia."

"You're a long ways from home," he said with a creepy smile.

The guy seemed nice enough, but he was a stranger in a foreign part of the country I'm not familiar with. I reminded myself not to mind his scraggly look. People in this part of the country are much friendlier.

He coughed, sounding like he would cough up a lung, the poor man. He watched me closely, coughing uncontrollably through his words. "It's okay. You don't need to be afraid of me. I couldn't hurt a fly."

I wasn't sure how much longer before another car would drive by, so I decided to trust the man.

***

The man was very friendly. He returned Mary and me to our stranded car, honked his horn, waved and drove away. I must remind myself to stop judging people by their appearance.

"Can you unlock the doors, Isabella?" Mary asked, pulling the door handle.

I reached into my pockets, but they were empty. I rummaged through my purse, but the keys weren't there either.

"You sure you didn't grab the keys when you were waiting in the car?" I asked as I peered through the window. They weren't laying on the seat or had fallen on the floor.

Mary looked through the passenger window. "I don't have the keys." She straightened up with panic in her eyes.

"What is it?"

"The keys are in the ignition."

I sprinted to the other side of the car and peered through the window. "You've got to be kidding me! I can't believe this is happening! First, I lose you at the airport, and we miss our flight. Then the flight we were supposed to be on crashes with no survivors. We get a flat tire, run out of gas and now lock the keys in the car with no phone service and are out in the middle of nowhere. It's like something doesn't want us here. Everything we do goes wrong."

BACK TO THE DAILY GRIND
(BELLA)

Beep, Beep, Beep, Beep.

I rolled over and hit the snooze button. I swear I got maybe three hours of sleep last night. I definitely could use another five. My eyes were heavy and sore, and my head pounded in my skull, and my throat felt scratchy, like sandpaper. I smacked my dry, cracked lips and grabbed the water bottle from my nightstand. I drained the entire bottle within seconds. It felt like a hangover from Hell, but I haven't had a drink in over six months.

Everything had been skewed lately. The trip to South Dakota, my sleep, I hardly eat anything, my body went through some intense changes for no apparent reason. My week off from work was supposed to be relaxing, however it had been anything but.

I couldn't complain too much. Once we reached Astoria, it was quiet and peaceful, much different from the city. Life in the Midwest was simple, with endless miles of farmland and cornfields—the country life I could get used to. It was a breath of fresh air. It would be a culture shock, but one I would embrace with open arms.

Now I was back to the daily grind and the hectic chaos that permeated this city, a daily reminder this town had forever changed. Everyone whispered and looked behind their backs, wondering when the next murder would take place. I think what frightened people the most was the police had no leads, and the killer was on the loose. But, to have a somewhat sane existence, I must push the negativity toward the back of my busy mind and try to live a positive life through this.

My dental practice soared to new heights, and we couldn't keep up with the new patient demand. It was amazing but hectic and stressful at the same time. I should have never taken the time off from work, but I had desperately needed a break. I think it had done me some good, to clear my head. The possibilities were endless for my career— financial stability and the opportunity to meet lots of new people who could possibly become more than just a familiar face.

Bang, Bang, Bang.

The loud thuds from the front door startled me. I leapt from bed.

BANG, BANG, BANG!

"Who the hell could be banging on my door at seven o'clock in the morning?" I unlocked the door and opened it. "Dad, what's wrong?"

"I've been trying to call your phone for over an hour."

"My phone is still on Silent. I just woke up."

"It's Mary!"

"What's wrong?"

"The police found her wandering the streets at four this morning."

"What?"

"She was lost. Didn't know where she was. Doesn't even remember her own name."

"Oh, no! Great-grandma had been calling me *Natalie*, but her memory just went like that?"

"I guess. It just doesn't make any sense. Did anything happen on your trip that might've been overly upsetting?"

"Not that I can think of. Overall, we had a good trip. It didn't start out fantastic by any means. Everything that could go wrong, went wrong. But, by the time we made it to Astoria, the rest of the world just seemed to disappear. All our worries and complications just vanished and was replaced with peace and tranquility. It was actually quite relaxing, much different than city life. Dad, do you think Great-grandma hates the city and would rather live in South Dakota? Could the stress cause her to lose her mind?"

"I'm not sure, sweetie, but it's certainly a possibility. All I know is that she's too old to be on her own. She needs us now more than ever, and we need to be there for her every step of the way."

"Of course, Dad."

"I think we should discuss this tonight over dinner with Rachel. Why don't you meet us at the house at seven?"

"Sure thing. I'll be there."

"See you tonight then." Dad gave a half smile, turned and walked away.

I exhaled a big sigh then proceeded to my mailbox by the edge of the busy road. Since I had been away for a week, I was sure it'd be full of unwanted mail that will most likely get thrown in the trash. I used my hand as a shield from the bright sunrays that blinded me. The grass between my toes—once tickling my delicate bare feet—now felt weathered, like worn leather cracking at the seams.

I thumbed through the pile of letters, but only one caught my eye. I ripped it opened, unfolded it and scanned it as my gaze darted from left to right. Besides a couple bills, the others I threw in the trash. The letter I had opened had some personal information, so I shredded it. I'm definitely paranoid. But who isn't nowadays?

***

"Dr. Williams, it's so nice to see you again. How was your trip to the Midwest?" Monica beamed as I approached the receptionist desk to my office. Monica was short and petite with dark hair pulled into a ponytail, revealing her high forehead and mole in the corner of her eye.

"Monica, you don't have to address me so formally. You can call me by my first name. It was very nice actually." I smiled. "How did things go while I was gone?"

"We were swamped! The phones have been ringing off the hook with new patients every day. We just can't seem to keep up. We have six people waiting, and Cindy called out sick today."

"It's okay, Monica. I'll handle it. Thanks for all your help."

"Isabella …"

I turned around.

Monica offered a coffee cup. "I made your coffee just the way you like it."

"Thank you, Monica. Another cup will do me good. I need the extra caffeine this morning."

***

My mind wandered all day, thinking about Carrie. I hadn't talked to her in so long. I wondered how she was doing. Last I heard, she had moved to California with Chad and their daughter, Chloe. Chloe must be seven now, so that would put her in ... second grade, I think. I really missed Carrie; she was my best friend. After she graduated and moved away, we just drifted apart. I should visit her in California sometime. What was I thinking? I had just returned from a trip, and we were busier than hell at the office. I couldn't leave anytime soon.

I missed having someone to confide in. I told Carrie things I'd never spoken of before. We had a crazy friendship. She was popular and loved to party, and I was quiet and love to read. We were complete opposites, but it worked. I trusted her, and she trusted me. She got married, had a kid and everything changed. Life changes us, I supposed.

I didn't lock up for the day until after six o'clock. We accepted twenty-four new patients today, and I was beat. I could crawl into bed and sleep for twelve hours straight, but I supposed I better stop by the bakery and buy some brownies for dessert at Dad's tonight. The bakery made the best brownies around. My favorite were the German chocolate ones. The frosting was rich and gooey with coconut and chopped pecans. Pure deliciousness, but they were dangerous, packed with tons of calories and fat. Most definitely a temptation hard to resist.

As I traversed Main Street, I noticed business owners had decorated all their store windows for Halloween, my favorite holiday. I loved all the creepy decorations—ghosts, scarecrows, bats, spiders, webs, blood, and anything scary. We had even decorated my office. We had gone all out, hanging stuff from the ceiling and walls and using motion-detected creatures with red eyes and faintly playing creepy music in the background. I loved all the pranks people pull on one another this time of year, trying to scare the bejeezus out of everyone. But this year was much different than the rest. No one was in the mood to scare each other, with the murders and all, which I could understand, but it was depressing. Everyone was so serious all the time. I wished people would just lighten up a little bit and try to have fun.

An old house built circa 1820 stood on top of a hill, overlooking the entire town. The property owner had turned it into a haunted house. It was too rundown for habitation, but it had been in his family for almost two centuries. Rumor had it the place was really haunted. They had some TV crew investigate the property years ago to capture any activity in that house, but the show never aired. Rumors had it that it had been too damn scary for the public's eyes, and one of the crew members had ended up in a mental institution after the investigation. They said the man had gone crazy.

It was the best haunted house I had ever been to. It knocked all the others clear out of the water by far. But, now that I think of it, maybe it was because the house was actually haunted and not a hoax that just seemed fake and overexaggerated, like most.

I remembered once I had walked by, and something flew off the shelf just inches from hitting me, freaking me out. I distinctly heard a child laughing and running up and down the stairs, but no one was there. And I recalled all the distant whispers and echoes in the house, and the floors and doors creaked, and lights flickered. The house was always cold too. It sent a chill to the bone, making all the hairs stand up. It was frightening, but that's what I enjoyed about it.

Being scared was an adrenaline rush, and I loved it. There was nothing quite comparable.

***

Dinner at Dad's was nice. Rachel cooked a pot roast dinner. The meat was always juicy and tender, never dry, and melted right in my mouth. She made the best gravy too, thick and bursting with flavor. I must admit Rachel was a great cook, and I loved visiting for dinner.

After much discussion, we decided the best option for Mary would be home healthcare. Dad would never let her go to a nursing home. A nurse would come by every day to check on her, wash her sheets, start a load of laundry, clean dishes, tidy the house, and take out the trash. Between Dad, Rachel and I, we could grab her groceries or bring her homecooked meals, if she didn't want to join us.

E. A. Owen

My Beautiful Wife

(Trevor)

I stepped outside and gazed at the sky. To my amazement, five bright full moons casted shadows of warning. Every moon gradually grew bigger in unison and then slowly faded, revealing millions of stars that freckled the darkness. Night turned to day in a blink of an eye.

How could this be happening? I stood shocked and confused. A strong gust of wind whipped around me, as if I was in the eye of a tornado. The storm destroyed my surroundings, shattering everything into pieces as objects float past me. Then everything froze, as if someone pressed Pause—time stood still. I spun slowly in awe at the phenomena, and, just as quickly as it froze, everything crashed down around me.

I gasped. It felt like I had been holding my breath for several minutes. I sat upright in bed—confused and drenched in sweat. *What a strange dream.* Much different than the recurring dream I'd had of the unknown chasing me and the fear that devours my soul. Dream interpretation had always intrigued me, especially the crazy, absurd dreams that just make absolutely no sense. I found it fascinating how the unconscious mind continued working even during sleep. And why did such unrealistic dreams seem so intense and real at the time, but, when awake, I'd wonder how in a million years I ever thought just for a second it could be real.

I shook my head and realized how badly I needed a cup of coffee. A shot of expresso would do, to add that extra jolt of caffeine I most definitely needed. Or better yet, a shot of rum in my coffee would be nice. Might get rid of this nasty headache. *Probably just dehydrated.* I walked to the fridge and poured a glass of orange juice and guzzled every last drop within seconds. Now that was refreshing.

I leaned over the kitchen sink and gazed out the window overlooking the backyard, staring at the massive overgrown maple trees that rose nearly one hundred feet. Its branches stretched in every direction with the most brilliant colorful leaves. It was picture perfect, something I'd see framed in an art gallery or adorning on a postcard or highlighted in calendar. It was full of character and life. The colors were amazing and beautiful with shades of pumpkin, crimson, and hints of lemon.

Autumn was my favorite season by far. It was absolutely beautiful this time of year, with all the changing colors. The foliage was breathtaking. I'd always thought how strange the cycle of nature was, especially autumn when everything started to die but how beautiful that transition was. Also, I cherished looking forward to the holidays with family. I loved Thanksgiving—the only time of year I could stuff my face with all the delicious food and not feel guilty. I looked forward to enjoying the foods we don't eat all year, like smoked turkey, stuffing, cranberry sauce, and my favorite, eggnog and pumpkin pie. But, to be honest, my favorite was garlic mashed potatoes with thick, creamy homemade gravy made from scratch. I must admit, gravy definitely makes the meal, with its saltiness and rich flavors that melt in the mouth with all its goodness. Just thinking about it made me hungry.

"You couldn't sleep either, honey?" Rachel asked quietly from behind me.

"No. I'm sorry. Did I wake you, sweetheart?"

"I woke up and noticed you weren't next to me. Is everything okay, Trevor?"

"Yeah, of course. I just had a crazy dream and didn't want to wake you. These strange dreams I've been having … just make no sense. They must have some sort of meaning behind them?"

"It's been a stressful couple of months. Everyone is acting paranoid. Life just isn't the same anymore since the murders. Of course your mind would play tricks in your dream world."

"I suppose you're right."

"How are you dealing with everything? The long days at work, being surrounded by negativity twenty-four/seven?"

"It's not bad all the time, especially when I come home to you every night." Rachel smiled.

I leaned in for a kiss. "I hope they catch the killer soon, so we can get back to normalcy. I'm so sick of all the whispering and people hiding behind closed doors, afraid to come out."

"When's the last time you checked on Mary? Sorry to change the subject."

"A couple days ago. She seems to be doing fine. This home health care makes a big difference. She has company on a daily basis—cleaning, preparing her meals, and making sure she takes her meds every day. But I've noticed how differently she acts now. I don't even think she knows who I am. She looks lost all the time. It's so sad to just watch her slowly losing her mind, dwindling away to nothing. Isabella said she keeps calling her *Natalie*. I'm just glad she hasn't wandered off again. "

"I can't imagine what she is going through. It must be so scary for her. Not knowing her own family or where she is half the time. It makes my heart weep. Mary was such a happy, lively woman, even after all the horrible things she has been through. She doesn't even want to spend time with us anymore. It's like we're strangers."

"I think she feels embarrassed and ashamed, so that's why she stays away. Are you hungry?"

"Yeah, starved."

"How does blueberry pancakes, fried eggs, and sausage sound?"

"Delicious."

***

I glance at the clock. *Just enough time to shower and fool around before we both head out for work.*

I know how to get Rachel in the mood too. She's not much of a morning person, or should I say, doesn't enjoy doing it early in the morning. But we need to be more affectionate and spontaneous. Our sex life has gone downhill with everything happening. We just haven't been in the mood, I guess.

"Why don't you freshen up," I whispered in her ear as I slowly placed gentle kisses down her neck.

Rachel looked at me with *that* look. She slowly licked her lips and bit her bottom lip with seduction behind her crystal-blue eyes. She let out a playful giggle and ran from the room.

I sprinted to the guest bathroom and showered, excitedly thinking of all the things I could do to Rachel. My beautiful wife has been so down lately, and I want to put a smile on her she can't wipe off. Or better yet, maybe I should just tease her and let her know what's in store for her when she comes home tonight. Get her all excited with intense anticipation for a night of romance and pure ecstasy. All these amazing thoughts danced around in my head.

I stepped from the steaming shower and dried my wet body with a towel. I walked down the hallway donning a stupid ear-to-ear grin. I slowly opened our bedroom door. Rachel stood by the bed in just a towel—and dropped it, revealing her sexy, naked, toned body.

She gave me a very provocative look, and I couldn't resist. I dropped my towel and threw her on the bed, passionately kissing her soft lips as I slid my hand, slowly separating her legs and growing rock hard myself. I slowly licked her as she moaned and arched her back. She tasted sweet.

She grabbed the blankets underneath her in a tight fist and twisted them as her body squirmed. I worked my magic until she was dripping wet. I crawled between her legs and thrusted myself inside her warm body as she releases a moan that would make any man cum in seconds.

Her eyes rolled to the back of her head as I thrusted deeper. She raised her legs straight into the air as I got her off several times before I orgasmed. I collapsed on the bed next to her trembling body.

Rachel smiled and pulled me in for an intense kiss. "I love you so much, Trevor."

"I love you too, baby," I reply, breathing rapidly and trying to catch my breath.

Rachel snuggled up to me with her leg on top of mine and her fingers gently caressing my chest and arm as she looks into my eyes—her cheeks flushed, hair a mess, seeming more beautiful than ever.

I kissed her forehead and ran my fingers through her long hair, thinking how lucky I was. Rachel was truly amazing. I'd never loved someone so deeply. She completed me.

MARY

(TREVOR)

I walked out the front door and locked it behind me. An uneasy feeling overcame me. *Mary!* I darted around the house and toward the guest house. Everything around me slowed down, and my feet grew heavy. My breathing echoed loudly in my head.

Bang, Bang! No answer.

All I heard was my heartbeat throbbing in my head.

Bang, Bang, Bang!

I frantically searched any signs of disturbance, but nothing seemed out of place. I tried to peer through her window, but the blinds were shut. I ran to the clothesline, lifted the top of the pole, pulled off the key attached to the other side, ran to the door and unlocked it.

"Mary!" I pushed through the door but heard nothing but stillness. I noticed how clean her place was, now that she has homecare. It was never like Mary to let the place get so filthy, but she hadn't been herself lately.

I heard faint music coming from her bedroom—sad cello music. I slowly pushed open her door. It creaked, but Mary didn't move. She lay on her side, a quilt pulled to her neck. All I could see was her long silver hair.

I approached her bed and whispered, "Mary," shaking her shoulder. "Mary."

I pulled her shoulder toward me to look at her face; it was pale. I gasped as I touched her cold skin. I felt for a pulse—nothing. A tear fell, rolling down my cheek.

She was all I had left of the biological family I never knew... And there was the deep, dark secret that Isabella and I were the only descendants left of the notorious Jack the Ripper. Why would I be thinking of such horrible thoughts?

Isabella is going to be devastated.

***

"Dad, what are you doing here?" I asked concerned as I removed my dental gloves and dropped them in the trashcan beside me.

"I've been calling and texting you all morning."

"I forgot my phone at home. What's going on?"

Dad dropped his head and wouldn't look me in the eye.

"Dad, what's wrong?" I lightly grabbed his shoulder and led him toward one of the empty rooms for privacy and closed the door behind us. I could tell by the way he was acting that I better take a seat. I sat in the dental chair and grabbed his hands in mine. "*Dad?*"

"It's—It's Mary. She's—"

"Dad! What's wrong with Great-grandma? Did she get lost again?"

Dad covered his face with shaky hands and sobbed. I stood and helped him sit in the chair and placed my hand on his shoulder.

"It's okay, Dad," I replied gently, trying to comfort him. *Knock, knock, knock.*

"Hold on. Give us a minute," I shouted behind the closed door. "Dad, what's wrong with Mary?"

"I —I had a bad feeling, so I ran to the guest house. Mary was lying in bed—still. But she wasn't sleeping. Her skin was cold and pale."

"Dad, what are you trying to say? Is Great-grandma dead?"

Tears streaked his cheeks.

My heart felt like it had been twisted and ripped from my chest. My soul—empty.

***

I was very close to Great-grandmother. I used to have sleepovers at her house when I was younger. We would do makeovers. She would paint my nails, put makeup on me, and curl my hair, and she would let me do the same to her. Except I wasn't very good at it, and we would giggle. We had so much fun. Mary said that when her mother was still alive, it was what she remembered most, and she wanted to pass those wonderful memories to me.

But what I remembered most was curling up beside her as she read books to me until I fell asleep. Because of Mary, I became obsessed with books and reading. It was a way I could escape into an imaginary world and completely lose myself. It was addicting and quite exhilarating. I read hundreds of books every year, taking me only a couple hours to finish a three-hundred-page book. Dad even turned the largest room in our house into a library. The shelves were built into the walls and stretch to the twenty-five-foot ceiling. Dad and Grandpa built a rolling ladder, so I could reach the books all the way at the top. My library held over five thousand books. I've probably only read about half of them. I had a real problem. I tended to buy more books before I finished reading the ones I already had. I couldn't visit Barnes & Noble without leaving with at least five to six books. A local bookstore sat just outside of town, with hundreds of books signed by the author, which is pretty awesome. I followed some of my favorite authors on social media, and when they come within a few hours from here, I liked to attend their book signings and meet them in person. I wished I could write a book, but I just don't have the patience or dedication. I got distracted easily, and my mind would wander. But reading was different. I just read what had already been written by a brilliant, creative mind. I don't have to think, just read. When I got lost in thought, it scared me. Sometimes I wondered if something was wrong with me, if I needed help. But who wasn't a little crazy?

I noticed what I was doing, trying to avoid what Dad had just told me. I breathed heavy; the room seemed to shift and go in and out of focus; I stumbled backward, catching myself on a nearby wall.

This can't be happening. It's not true. Dad—Dad is mistaken. I slid down the wall and sat on the floor. *Mary was just in a deep sleep. She was having a good dream and didn't want to be wakened. She's just fine. You'll see.* The thoughts continued, sounding a little convincing. *I'll go over there tonight, and she'll be sipping tea in her rocking chair, watching the sunset like she loves to do. We'll sit outside, gazing up in awe at the beautiful display of colors painted across the darkening sky.*

"Isabella? Are you okay, sweetheart?"

I snapped back into reality. "I don't know, Dad. I'm just trying to wrap my head around this."

"It's going to be okay, Bella. We're going to be okay." Dad stammered, trying to regain his composure. "Mary lived a long life. She would have been eighty-two years old next month. Mary has been through more heartache than anyone I know. She deserves to be at peace now."

THERAPY
(BELLA)

"I've never been to a funeral before. I've never lost anyone I love until now. My mom died during childbirth, but I didn't know her. As hard as it's been to grow up without a mom, I don't know any different. It was probably better this way. The pain and ache I feel inside is tearing me apart. I have no idea how Great-grandma could move on after so many deaths.

"First, her parents tragically died in a car accident when she was just twelve years old. I couldn't imagine, and I'm twenty-three. You're probably wondering how I graduated from dental school so quickly. First off, I graduated high school early at sixteen, and it took me just six years in college, taking accelerated classes, of course, to achieve my doctorate degree. I've been at my practice for almost a year now, and we're so busy that we can't keep up with the demand. I apologize, I got sidetracked again. Sorry.

"So, Mary lost both her parents when she was twelve, her husband after fifteen years of marriage, her daughter less than a year later, and her granddaughter which she never met, since both my dad and his sister were put up for adoption right after they were born. My dad didn't even know he had a sister, so he never got to meet her before she died either—so sad.

"Dad contacted all of Great-grandma's brothers and sister. They flew out for the funeral and stayed a few days before flying back. I had met all of them when Mary and I went to her old stomping grounds just a few weeks ago. I'm glad I met them and spent some one-on-one time with her before she passed. Mary, being the oldest, isn't far ahead of them in age. Angel is the youngest, and she's seventy-three. They all promised to keep in contact after the funeral."

"So, how long has it been since the funeral, Isabella?" Dr. Marshall asked.

"It's been about six months probably."

"What made you decide to come see me?"

"The pain has just become so unbearable. I can't concentrate at work. The other day, when I was filling a patient's tooth, my hand slipped when my mind wandered and cut his lip wide open. He needed four stitches. I felt horrible."

"Death can be really hard on people, especially when it affects their wellbeing."

"I can't sleep, and, when I do, I have these horrible dreams. Dreams that frighten me. I think something is wrong with me, Doctor."

"Do you ever do anything fun? I mean, to get your mind off work and your great-grandma's death?"

"No, not really. I don't have any friends. I'm a workaholic. I spend all my free time reading. It's my way to escape reality. I learned to love reading when I was five. My great-grandma moved into our guesthouse shortly after my heart transplant, so she could be closer to us. She missed seeing my dad grow up, since he had been put up for adoption after he was born, so she didn't want to miss that with me too. Mary and I had a very close relationship. I would have sleepovers at her house often. We'd do makeovers just like her mom used to do with her, and, of course, she'd read to me all the time. She'd get into character, change her tone with each character, and make lots of facial expressions whether it was happy or sad or mad or surprised—you get it. She was very theatrical, and I loved it. My dad tried reading to me, but it just wasn't the same. He wouldn't read with the emotion behind the words, like Mary would. She made reading fun."

"Would you say your great-grandma was your best friend?"

I smiled. "Now that I think of it like that, yes … Yes, she was."

"I can see why you're having a hard time dealing with her death, Isabella. She meant the world to you. Didn't she?"

"More than you know."

"I've learned a lot in our first session. I think it'd be best if we met again next week. Why don't you make an appointment with Amy on your way out? I'd like to talk more about these dreams you've been having lately, to see if I need to prescribe medication for you to sleep better. Without a good night's sleep, it'd be hard for you to stay focused at work, and you may have another accident, and we don't want that to happen again."

"No, of course not. That was awful. I'll make an appointment for next week. Thank you, Dr. Marshall."

"You can call me Joe." He grinned as he stood and extended his hand.

I noticed his strong grip.

"Hold on. Let me grab you something." He approached a cabinet on the other side of the room and unlocked it. He grabbed something and handed it to me. "I want you to take one of these an hour before you plan on going to bed every night until we meet again. Let me know if these help you sleep any better."

I examined the box. "I will. Thank you, Joe."

"Please don't drink any alcohol or drive when you take these either."

"I won't." I smiled, turned and left the room.

***

I couldn't stop thinking about Dr. Marshall. He stood about 5'9", with dirty-blond hair, striking blue eyes, and a five-o'clock shadow. He was very handsome and probably ten years older than me. I didn't notice a wedding ring, so he must not be married, but that didn't mean he wasn't taken. I didn't notice any pictures of a significant other or kids, but maybe he was not one of those to flaunt his family in his line of business, since things could get pretty personal in his office. Maybe he didn't want his clients asking questions.

I was twenty-three and had never been on a date before. I know, I know—sad and pathetic. But I'd been too busy to think about being with someone. I just didn't have the time, but I sure could daydream.

E. A. Owen

THE
ACCIDENT
(BELLA)

Copious amounts of dark crimson blood was splattered in every direction. *How did I get here?* I grabbed my head, the pain radiating. Disoriented, I stumbled and tripped over something, landing on my hands and knees. It was a body— or what was left of him.

His face was unrecognizable, marred with deep lacerations. A screwdriver was lodged into his eye socket. His nose and ears were sawed off, leaving only jagged pieces of skin.

Who would do such a thing?

The stench of rotten meat hung in the air. I felt nauseated. Panicked, I stood slowly and stepped backward before turning and running from the slaughter room.

This was just one of my many horrible dreams. Since taking the sleeping pills Dr. Marshall had prescribed me, my dreams have become more frequent and vivid. Normally, I would awaken abruptly from a dead sleep, breathing heavily and drenched in sweat, the horrible images fading shortly after. But now, the ugly scene was forever etched in my mind like a fingerprint.

I stepped from the hot shower and dried myself. I wiped the foggy mirror, leaving handprint streaks, and stared at my distorted reflection. *What is wrong with me?* I must remind myself it's for the best; they'll see. I know I've been stressed lately, and the loss of Great-grandmother weighs a lot on my fragile mind. The thoughts invading my conscious mind were disturbing and terrified me, as for the reason I thought talking to a therapist might help me, but I may have a slight crush, and I wouldn't want to taint him with my distorted, dark soul. But, deciphering my dreams was more important than what a man I had just met thought of me. I needed help, and I didn't know who else to ask. Besides, state law's doctor-patient confidentiality protected me. But what was I afraid of? I hadn't done anything wrong. I just had some disturbing dreams I couldn't interpret. Maybe it was normal, but I didn't think so. Something might be seriously wrong with me, and I wanted to get to the bottom of it.

I finished getting ready and grabbed my keys. I gazed at the clear blue sky as beautiful songbirds perched in the maple tree missing half its leaves. I shuddered. The cool breeze reminded me that autumn was almost over, and winter would be approaching soon. Luckily, Virginia didn't get much snow, but I would love for a white Christmas this year. I couldn't remember the last time we had a white Christmas. I had been a kid, so it had been a long time.

I turned my car's ignition—nothing. I try again.

"You've got to be kidding me," I muttered, slamming my fists on the steering wheel. *The office is only a few miles away, and it's the perfect day for a walk.*

I returned inside, grabbed a light jacket and headed out. I took my phone from my pocket and dialed the office. "Hi,

Monica. My car won't start, so I'll be late today. I've decided to walk and enjoy the weather. Please have Erica start the appointments, and I'll be in as soon as I can."

***

After thirty minutes of walking, I noticed a Starbuck's sign in the distance and thought I should treat myself. As I approached, I noticed the full parking lot, and the drive-thru lane had six cars in queue. I entered and stood fourth in line. I fumbled through my purse to find my wallet, and I located my Starbuck's punch card. The card was full. It was my lucky day—a free beverage.

I approached the counter, and a strawberry-blonde young girl—with loose curls just past her shoulders, high cheekbones kissed with freckles, and wide green eyes—patiently waited for me to place my order.

"I'll take a mocha peppermint latte with skim milk."

She rolled her eyes, annoyed. "What size?"

"Grande, please."

"That comes to $5.11." She wouldn't even look me in the eyes when she spoke.

I proceeded to hand her my punch card.

She sighed and snatched it from my hands.

She must be having a bad day.

"You can wait over there," she said frustrated, pointing to the other side of the counter. "It'll be just a few minutes. We're shorthanded today."

I grabbed a ten-dollar bill from my wallet and stuffed it into her tip jar.

The girl looked up and smiled. "Thank you!"

I returned the smile and approached the other side of the counter. I noticed the girl's attitude changed with the next customer.

She wore a smile and looked them in the eyes while talking.

I realized the smallest gesture could change someone's day. I always reminded myself that I had no idea what someone else was going through. They could have lost a loved one, recently filed for a divorce or had declared bankruptcy, been fired from their job, or just learned they have cancer.

"Medium mocha peppermint latte," the barista hollered as he set my order on the counter.

I grabbed it and headed for the exit. I retrieved my phone and texted Dad. *My car wouldn't start this morning. I'm walking to work. If you have time today, could you please swing by and look at it?*

I glanced up, and my eyes widened in terror. I gasped as the force hit me like a ton of bricks. My bones crushed. I tumbled up the hood, smashing into the windshield. My body propelled into the air, then my skull cracked hard off the pavement as everything turned black.

BROKEN
(BELLA)

Disoriented and drifting in and out of consciousness, my eyelids slowly fluttered open, the florescent lights from above, blinded me. The throbbing in my skull was excruciating. I rubbed my forehead. I used all my strength and righted myself from a lying position, my body trembling. My entire body ached, resonating deep. It felt like I had been hit by a freight train.

I gasped, noticing both legs were in casts. My eyes darted frantically. I was in a hospital room. I noticed an older woman reading a book in a bed across the room.

"Excuse me," I whispered through dry, cracked lips. "Ex … excuse me," I said a little louder.

The lady looked from her book and toward me. "You're awake!"

"How—How long have I been here?"

"Two days. The nurse will want to know you're awake." She leaned over the side of the bed and pressed something.

"What—happened to me?"

"I overheard them talking. You got hit by a car."

"What?"

"Your mom and dad have visited a couple times."

"She's not my mom."

Knock, knock.

The door opened and a rotund lady with short dark hair, a chubby face, and a stubby nose entered. "Isabella, my name is Susan. I'm the nurse on duty. Glad to see you're awake. How are you feeling?"

"Like shit!"

"Well, that's expected."

I glanced at my casted legs. "How long do I have to wear these?"

"The doctor will have to explain the details with you. Would you like something to make you feel better?"

"Something strong."

"I'll be right back. I'll give your father a call and let him know you're awake." The lady waddled from the room and closed the door behind her.

I uncomfortably tried adjusting my body. It seemed like an hour had passed before the nurse reentered. She approached the bedside and handed me a tiny white paper cup containing two small round white pills imprinted with 54 733.

"This is morphine. These should help with the pain."

"Thank you." I took the cup and tipped the pills into my mouth as the nurse handed me a glass of water. I swallowed hard. I hated taking pills, but the pain was unbearable.

"I called your father. He said he'll be here in twenty minutes." Susan smiled and left the room again.

I hope these pills kick in soon.

***

I glanced across the room at the wall clock. Twenty minutes had passed. Where was Dad?

Knock, knock.

Dad peeked around the door as Rachel and he pushed through.

"Hi, Isabella. How are you feeling?"

"A little better. The nurse gave me some morphine. I was in a lot of pain when I woke up."

"I can only imagine. I'm so sorry, sweetheart."

"Does my office know what happened?"

"I let them know as soon as I found out. They cancelled all appointments except routine cleanings until you're well enough to go back to work. The doctor said it might be a week."

"Lovely!" I said sarcastically. "I just want to know when I can get these ugly things off."

"You broke them pretty bad, Bella. Most breaks take six to eight weeks to heal. Yours might take longer. You're lucky to be alive. That was a close call."

"What happened?"

"You were on your phone and walked into the road without looking. The driver didn't have time to react. You'll need to stay with me and Rachel until you can walk on your own again. The doctor said you'll need a wheelchair, since both your legs are broken. I or Rachel can drive you to and from work every day. It's going to be a rough few weeks, but we can manage."

"Thanks, Dad. Thanks, Rachel." I lowered my head and wiped a tear streaking my cheek.

A sharp pain shot up my leg and into my spine. I shrieked, grabbing my leg. This will be a miserable eight weeks.

DISTURBING DREAMS
(BELLA)

"After the accident, the nightmares stopped for a while. It was nice to get a good sleep, waking up well rested. The morphine helped with the pain, but, once I left the hospital, the doctor wouldn't give me a prescription, saying it had high risk for addiction and dependency. My body aches all over. The massive bruises are turning green now. The throbbing in my skull feels like my head is splitting in two. I've never experienced so much pain in my life."

Dr. Marshall just nodded as he jotted things in his notebook as I spoke. "What has been the hardest part for you, Isabella?"

"Not being able to walk or drive, and the stares I get every time I go anywhere. But most of all, not being able to visit my great-grandma, since she used to live in our guesthouse."

"How does that make you feel?"

"Sad and lonely. I used to talk to her about everything. I feel guilty, because, when I was in college, I didn't come home much, even though I was only an hour away. I made a new friend, Carrie, and we were inseparable. That is, until she got pregnant and married. She changed. I was her maid of honor. I haven't talked to her much since they moved to California. But that's probably mostly my fault."

"Why was it your fault?"

"Well, I got jealous and said some things that upset Carrie. So, we only communicate when we have to. It makes me sad. I told Carrie things I never told anyone before. I trusted her. We had a crazy friendship, but it worked."

"In what ways?"

"We were complete opposites. I was quiet and shy. I had my nose in a book all the time, studying and reading. Carrie was wild, loved to party, and, of course, was beautiful and popular."

"How did you meet?"

"We were roommates. I lost Carrie and now my great-grandma. I feel so alone." A hard lump formed in the back of my throat, making it hard to talk. I quickly wiped the tear streaking my cheek.

"Well, technically, you didn't lose Carrie. She just lives far away. You could always visit her sometime."

"That wouldn't be a good idea."

"Why not?"

"It's complicated." I shifted in my seat, unable to look him in the eyes. An awkward silence descended upon the room. I think the doctor realized the conversation made me uncomfortable.

"How did the sleeping pills I gave you a couple weeks ago work?" Dr. Marshall quickly changed the subject.

"Made my nightmares more frequent and intense."

"*Hmmm.* We can try something different this time. Could you describe one of your dreams?"

"Massive amounts of blood splattered everywhere. I tripped over a body—or what was left of him. It was horrifying. His face was unrecognizable—deep lacerations. The horrid stench of rotten meat hung in the air. I felt nauseated. I panicked and ran out of the room."

"I see." Dr. Marshall jotted frantically on his notepad.

I see? That's all he's going to say? I bit my nails. *He thinks I'm crazy, doesn't he?* My eyes dart frantically around the room. *What do I say? His silence is making me nervous.*

I broke the silence. "Why do I have these kinds of dreams? They always involve blood and dead bodies. Is this normal?"

"Our subconscious has always been a mystery. People have claimed they know what our dreams mean, but it's just a theory. Stress has a lot to do with strange dreams. Tragic events, like your accident, or the loss of someone close to us can certainly affect our dream world. You have experienced all of these, so I don't think it's abnormal for you to be having such violent nightmares."

"But I've had these types of dreams my entire life—as long as I can remember. Most of the time, after I wake up suddenly, I think I won't forget the dream, but, shortly after, it just magically erases from my memory. Once I took those pills you gave me, I can't get them out of my head. It's like they've been imprinted in my memories forever."

"It's up to you, but, if you want to learn more about your subconscious and your dreams, maybe you should take them a while longer. Write down your dreams in a journal and compare each dream, moving forward. Watch for similarities, if they get better or worse, and when. But it's completely up to you. Or we can try a different medication."

"My whole reason coming to you was to get to the bottom of these violent, disturbing dreams. I think something is seriously wrong with me, Dr. Marshall."

"Have you ever tried hypnosis?"

"No. Does it work?"

"Sometimes. Some people are more susceptible than others. It opens your subconscious, to remember things—events your brain has suppressed or doesn't want to remember. Our brain does an impeccable job to protect us from harmful events—a way, I guess, for us to move on with our lives and forget. Hypnosis might help. Maybe you forgot something from your childhood. That might help you, and maybe your dreams would stop. Maybe it's a warning. I'm not saying it *will* help, but it's worth a try, if you're willing."

I nodded.

"By the way, hypnosis works best if you're overtired. Makes you go under easier. Why don't you make an appointment for next week, and we can try the hypnotherapy then?"

"Sure."

"It was nice seeing you again, Isabella." Dr. Marshall smiled, approached my wheelchair and extended his hand.

"Nice seeing you too." I smiled, shook his hand and wheeled myself out.

No Explanation
(Bella)

A week had passed, and I was nervous about the hypnotherapy. Afraid about what I might discover. Did I really want to know the truth? Could Dr. Marshall be right? Has my brain suppressed my memories to protect me from something so awful that it's best I didn't find out? Was I strong enough to handle what my brain might unlock? I wasn't so sure. I started to have second thoughts. Maybe not knowing was for the best. Was I making the right decision? I was in a constant battle with myself. I better decide quickly; my appointment started in less than ten minutes.

I approached the receptionist desk, my hands sweaty from my nerves.

"Hi, Isabella. It's nice to see you. How are you feeling?" Amy asked with a concerned tone.

"I'm feeling better. Can't wait to get out of this wheelchair and walk and drive again."

"I'm sure that's got to be tough. Do you have to see a physical therapist once they remove the casts?"

"Three times a week, for two weeks, the doctor predicts. Or until my legs get strong enough."

"How much longer do you have?"

"The casts are scheduled to come off in five weeks, as long as all my bones have healed properly. I broke them badly, so I hope it doesn't take longer. It feels like I've had them on for six months."

"I bet. I can't imagine. How's the pain?"

"I get a sharp pain that shoots up my legs and into my spine sometimes. That's painful! Otherwise, not too bad for the circumstances. They are sore and ache. And boy, do they itch like crazy sometimes."

"Are you taking any medication for the pain?"

"Just Tylenol. Seems to take the edge off."

"You're a stronger woman than me. If I were in your shoes right now, they'd have to give me something stronger."

"At the hospital, they gave me morphine, but, because it's so highly addictive, my doctor wouldn't prescribe me any to take home. Which is fine with me. Morphine would be nice right now but not worth the risks."

"Yeah, I suppose you're right."

"I'm ready for Miss Williams." Dr. Marshall's voice came over the phone intercom.

"Dr. Marshall is ready to see you now."

I smiled and wheeled toward his office.

"Isabella, how are you feeling today?" Dr. Marshall stood from his desk as he spoke.

"I'm fine. Just a little sore. No headache today either, which is a first."

"That's good to hear. Are you still okay with our hypnotherapy session today?"

I bit my nails. "I don't know. I've been having second thoughts."

"That's normal. It can be a scary thought, digging into your subconscious. And it's perfectly fine if we postpone it for another time when you're more comfortable, Isabella."

I exhaled a long sigh. "No. I'm as ready as I'll ever be. Let's ... just get it out of the way. I need to know, even if I'm afraid."

"Okay. I need you to relax. Close your eyes, and listen to my voice," Dr. Marshall instructed in a calm, soothing tone. "Take a deep breath. Open your lungs ... ever ... so ... slowly. And exhale. Focus on your breathing. In .... and out. In ... and out. Imagine you're in a happy place. It's peaceful. And quiet. So quiet that you can hear a pin drop. You're calm and relaxed. You're free from pain and stress. Take a deep breath and hold it. Hold it ... Now slowly exhale as you feel it move down your neck. Down to your arms ... and into your fingertips. Take another deep breath. As you exhale, feel it moving down your neck ... into your chest ... to your stomach. Now your legs and into your toes. Good ... Do you feel relaxed?"

I slowly nodded, listening intently to his voice.

***

Awakening from the trancelike state, my eyelids felt heavy. I closed my eyes and blinked hard, everything refocusing. Streaks of sunlight penetrated the darkened room. My muscles felt weak as I reluctantly sat upright, outstretching my arms a big yawn escaped my cracked lips. I felt as if I had been in a deep sleep for twelve hours.

A feeling of confusion overwhelmed me. *Where am I?*

That's when I saw terror in Dr. Marshall's eyes.

"What ... What happened?"

"Do you remember anything, Isabella?"

"No. What happened?"

"You were under hypnosis for a while. How are you feeling?" Dr. Marshall shifted uncomfortably in his chair, unable to look me in the eyes.

"Actually, I feel great. Feels like I slept twelve hours straight. I haven't felt this good in a long time."

"And your pain?"

"Gone. It's amazing."

"I'd assume you'll feel like this for the next few hours. But, unfortunately, the pain will return."

"This is absolutely fantastic! When can we do this again?"

Dr. Marshall's gaze nervously darted around the room.

"Did it work? I don't remember anything. It's weird."

Dr. Marshall cleared his throat. "I'm afraid to tell you, but I won't be able to see you again."

My eyes grew wide, and I swallowed the lump in my throat. "Why?"

"I wouldn't suggest trying hypnotherapy again, Isabella. Some things are just best left alone."

"But, Dr. Marshall ..."

"It's to protect you, Isabella. I take doctor-patient confidentiality very seriously, but my conscious is really telling me to do the right thing here," Dr. Marshall replied sternly.

"But ... I don't understand! What happened? What did I say?"

"It's best if you leave my office now, Isabella." Dr. Marshall opened his office door.

"I'm sorry."

I wheeled myself out, my cheeks wet.

***

After Dr. Marshall had banished me from his office, I'd become unstable. I couldn't believe he just left me hanging like that, with no explanation. I'd already had a hard enough time dealing with the death of Great-grandmother and the accident; I definitely didn't need this added stress.

To escape, I'd usually drown myself in books, but even that I couldn't do anymore. I couldn't focus. My mind constantly revisited that day, trying to comprehend it. But all that remained was an empty hole, like my memory had been wiped clean. The harder I tried to remember, the worse I felt. I'd never felt so alone. My world darkened. I felt nothing but emptiness. The darkness consumed me, picking at me, piece by piece, 'til soon nothing would be left.

I stared at my reflection in the vanity mirror, an emptiness behind my eyes. I pushed down and twisted open the bottle of pills and tipped them down my throat as I grabbed the bottle of whiskey and took a big swig. Glancing back at my reflection, I smiled with so much meaning behind it, except happiness—a smile, disturbing and ugly, deep and powerful. A smile that said, *It's over, and I can finally rest in peace.*

9-1-1
(TREVOR)

My eyes flung open, and my breath quickened. The sheets stuck to my sweaty body. The oscillating fan sent chills down my spine. My heart felt like it would jump from my chest. A feeling of dread consumed my soul. Something didn't feel right. *Had it been a dream?*

A glimmer of moonlight danced on the walls. I glanced at my beautiful wife, sleeping so peacefully. Not wanting to wake her, I slid my legs over the bedside and tiptoed from the room. I slowly opened the door, as it creaks, then closed the door quietly behind me. Traversing the hallway, my feet felt cold against the marble floors.

I should have grabbed socks. I shrugged.

I flipped on the kitchen light and glanced at the wall clock—12:37.

That's it? I need to go back to bed! I poured a tall glass of orange juice—just a few gulps and it was gone. I wiped my mouth with the back of my hand. The feeling wasn't dissipating; it seemed to worsen.

I grabbed a bottle of Tylenol from the cabinet and swallowed two pills. I entered the living room, sat in the oversized leather recliner and kicked back, my legs extending on the footrest. Growing up, I remembered experiencing overwhelming unexpected feelings, but it had been many years now. Lightheaded and nauseated, I rubbed the back of my neck, closed my eyes and took a deep breath, holding it for a moment and exhaling slowly.

"What the hell is going on with me?" I mumble, rolling my neck side to side. "I hope this Tylenol kicks in soon." I yawned wide. "I'll just rest my eyes for a moment before I crawl back in bed with my sleeping beauty."

"Isabella," a voice whispered.

Half asleep, I jolted awake. "Who said that?" I frantically scanned the room. "Bella!" I gasped, wide-eyed.

I sprinted upstairs to Bella's room. As I approached her bedroom door, I slowed my pace.

Knock, knock.

I wait a moment; it was too quiet.

Knock, knock, knock.

Still nothing. I turned the doorknob, hoping she hadn't locked it. *Thank goodness.* I pushed quietly through the door.

"Bella?" I whispered, tiptoeing toward the shadow of her bed. "Bella …" I whispered louder.

I felt a light breeze from the open window as the curtain rippled in a rhythmic pattern, and the moonlight cast shadows in the room. I could barely decipher her body's outline, bundled up underneath the blankets.

I shook her shoulder. "Bella!"

Something didn't feel right. I ran to flip on the light. Then I noticed it—an open pill bottle on Isabella's vanity, fallen onto its side.

I examined the bottle. "Catheryn Jacobs?" I recited in confusion. "Hydrocodone, ten milligrams … *No!*"

I dashed to Isabella's side and shook her hard, trying to wake her, but she was out cold. I quickly charged to the bathroom, filled a red Solo cup by the sink faucet and splashed water into her face—not a flinch. I patted my thighs, but all I wore were boxers. That's when I spotted Bella's cellphone on the ground next to her vanity.

I swiped the screen to unlock it. *What has she done?* I panicked as I tried to steady my hands enough to dial 9-1-1. *Time is of the essence. An ambulance will never get here in time.* I dropped the phone and slid one arm behind Isabella's neck and the other behind her knees, grunting as I stood. Bella was small, but dead body weight and her casts weighed her down, I swear adding an extra fifty pounds.

I ran down the stairs through the dark, losing my balance and almost tripping. I gently laid Isabella on the couch and sprinted to my bedroom. I swung open the door and flipped on the light.

"Rachel, honey. Wake up," I said, frantically getting dressed.

"Wha ... What's wrong?" Rachel moaned half asleep.

"It's Bella. She ... She took a bottle of pills. I have to get her to the hospital."

"She what? I'm coming with." Rachel sprung from bed and stumbled to her feet.

"Hurry! We don't have much time."

I darted back to Bella's side, wrapped my arms around her lifeless body and fireman-carried her through the front door, not bothering to close it, knowing Rachel would be right behind us. I struggled to balance Isabella's weight while trying to open the car's back door just as Rachel's hand appears. I moved back as Rachel opened it then stepped aside. I laid Isabella on the back seat and sped off, tires squealing and leaving behind the smell of burnt rubber.

My cheeks were wet. I raised my trembling hand to wipe the tears. Rachel put her hand on my leg and squeezed it, looking in my direction. I turned my face away.

"It'll be okay, Trevor. Bella will be okay," Rachel said gently with sorrow behind her eyes as she forced a half smile.

I sniffled and nodded, hoping she was right.

Raindrops splattered the windshield, making it hard to see. I hated driving at night in the rain. A flash of light illuminated the dark sky followed by a rumble in the distance. I had read somewhere once that lightning could reach as high as 50,000 degrees Fahrenheit, which is five times hotter than the surface of the sun. Mother Nature had always fascinated me. I had considered being a storm chaser once when I was in high school. I thought how exciting that job would be but figured it was just a fantasy and not a real job. I decided to be an engineer instead. I liked my job and was very good at it, but it was not something I ever got excited about.

BOOM!

I jolted, swerving into the other lane. White knuckling the steering wheel, I snapped back to reality as the violent downpour struck the windshield with amazing force.

"I can't see a thing!" I hunched over the steering wheel, squinting through the blanket of distorted images.

"Just pull over," Rachel pleads.

A noise from the back seat startled me. I turned the wheel slowly and came to complete stop. I flipped on the dome light, unbuckled my seatbelt and turned around.

Isabella violently convulsed. Her eyes blinked rapidly, slightly opened enough for me to see her eyes roll back in her head, drooling.

"Bella!"

E. A. Owen

SHREDDING MY INSIDES
(BELLA)

Not a cloud was in the sky. The sun's warmth kissed my skin as I ran in a field amongst beautiful flowers—roses, tulips, lilies, and daffodils. The colors looked raw and vibrant—reds, purples, pinks, and yellows. The view was breathtaking, as the sweet aroma filled the crisp, spring air.

Running, I looked at my legs. The casts were gone, the pain gone. I grinned, twirling and dancing on top of a wildflower hill. In the distance were mountains and a lake, resembling something from of a traveling magazine—a picture I wanted to take with me and mount on my walls forever. I spun with my arms extended, feeling the breeze against my delicate skin.

"Is … a … bel … la …" a soft voice echoed from afar.

I stopped and looked around. "Who's there?"

"Is … a … bel … la …"

I saw a familiar-looking lady approach. *Who is she?* I gasped. "Mom? Mom, is that you?"

She looked just like the picture I've had of her since I was a little girl—tall, slender, long honey-blond hair, fair skin, and hazel eyes. She was incredibly beautiful. Dad always said I look just like her, but, of course, I don't see it.

"Isabella," Mother said gently. "You have to wake up."

"But ... Mom. I've missed you so much. I have so much to say."

"You have to wake up, dear. It's not your time."

I ran to her and wrapped my arms around her, but her image faded. A tear rolled down my cheek. "Mom, wait. Please don't go," I whimpered. I fell to my knees; tears filled my eyes. I buried my face in my hands and sobbed uncontrollably. "Mom, please don't leave me. I need you!"

A force so strong hit me like a lightning bolt. My body flipped backward, and I hit the ground with a *thud*, knocking the wind from me, my chest burning. *What the hell is happening?* I gasped for air.

The force hit me again as I screamed in pain, my chest splitting apart. Everything around me faded into thick static. Disoriented and drifting in and out of consciousness, my eyelids slowly fluttered open, blinking rapidly, the florescent lights blinding me. A loud ringing echoed in my ears. I cringed and covered my ears.

Where am I? My gaze wandered aimlessly. The steady rhythm of simultaneous beeps from the heart monitor overpowered the ringing in my ears, and my chest rose and fell drastically with every deep breath I took.

"She's back," a deep-pitched voice proclaimed. "How are you feeling?"

I groaned an unintelligible response.

"We almost lost you there, Isabella," a heavyset man with whickers, deep-set eyes, and narrow lips replied. "Your heart stopped for twelve whole minutes. Thank God, you're still alive."

I rubbed my forehead, trying to relieve the throbbing in my skull.

"We've contacted a suicide-prevention specialist. You need to speak to her before you can go home. It's hospital procedure, and I won't sign your discharge papers until we feel comfortable you won't try harming yourself again." He rubbed the back of his neck and rolled his head from side to side. "You were having a seizure when your parents brought you in."

I rolled my eyes and crossed my arms as I listened to the fat doctor continue his little speech.

"This is serious, Isabella. You almost died. Your chest will be sore for the next couple days, since we had to shock your heart after you flatlined for several minutes, and CPR was not working. Some serious bruising will occur and possible fractures to your ribs. You're in rough shape." The doctor looked at my casts then handed me a cup. "I need you to drink this. It's activated charcoal. It'll coat your stomach. We had to pump your stomach when you arrived." He sighed, setting a bottle of water next to me. "I'm going to send in your parents. They're waiting to see you." He jammed his hands in his scrub pocket, turned and left the room.

I looked in the cup. It was a thick black substance. *Gross!* I pinched the brim of my nose and gulped it down as fast as I could, gagging a few times. It tasted horrible, like chalky cement. *Disgusting!* I grabbed the water bottle and twisted off the top. I gulped almost the entire contents. I just couldn't wash the taste from my mouth.

Knock, knock.

The door slowly opened, and Dad peaked around the corner with an expression full of sadness. "Hi, sweetheart." His lower lip trembled. "How are you feeling?"

I hated seeing my Dad this way. I couldn't imagine how upset and disappointed he was in me. I was selfish as hell and had just tried ending my life.

I looked at my hands, trying to avoid eye contact. "I'm so sorry, Dad."

"I hope you know you can talk to me about anything, honey." He sniffled as a single tear streaked his cheek. He raised his hand and wiped it. "Anything!"

Shame shredded my insides as my throat tightened, tears falling like rain. I sobbed, unable to speak.

"I can't lose you, Bella. You mean everything to me." He approached me and wrapped his arms around my body as he buried his face in my shoulder.

We hugged, crying in each other's arms, my tears soaking his shirt.

"I love you, Isabella."

"I love you too, Dad," I replied, sobbing uncontrollably.

BAD DAY
(BELLA)

A few months had passed, and the doctor had finally removed my casts. I saw a therapist once a week after my suicide attempt, but I decided therapy wasn't for me, so I stopped going. She was always telling me, "I know what you're going through Isabella." Seriously? She had no idea. Just some cliché response. It was just like a therapist saying they know what it was like to go through drug withdrawals and how hard it was, when they had never touched a drug in their life. Please! No books, research, or school could teach them. Without firsthand experience and that street knowledge, they couldn't know anything. I wished they didn't pretend. They weren't inside my head, so they had no clue what I was going through.

After tossing and turning in bed for over an hour, I decided to get up. Besides, my alarm would go off in forty minutes anyway, might as well get an early start to the morning instead of rushing around, which I normally did, trying to catch those extra few minutes of shuteye.

I started the coffeemaker and plopped onto the couch. I flipped through the channels until something caught my eye. I flipped back. The girl who had taken my latte order at Starbuck's right before the car had hit me was crying to the news reporter. I turned up the volume.

"A monster is walking the streets. Why haven't they caught him yet? If the police did their job, this maniac would be behind bars, and my dad would still be alive." She sobbed uncontrollably.

The camera panned to a reporter. "It's been several months since the last murder. Our community finally thought it might be safe again, but we were dead wrong. The killings have begun again. With the killer still on the loose, everyone needs to proceed with caution. Lock your doors, and don't go out alone at night. The police still haven't released any details on the murders—"

I turned off the TV. Mocking the reporter, I muttered, "Our community finally thought it might be safe again? *Huh!*"

Suddenly, it felt like the temperature dropped twenty degrees. I grabbed a hold of my arms and vigorously rubbed them. I looked around; all the windows were closed. *That's strange.* I scrunched my forehead.

That's when I remembered I had brewed a pot of coffee a few minutes ago. I opened the foyer closet and pulled the dark purple hoodie, with *Rocky Mountains* written across it, over my head. I hollered in pain, grabbing my foot and hopping on one leg. I fell over and hit my head on the side of the countertop. *Jesus Christ! What is wrong with me today?*

While pouring a cup of coffee, I burned my hand. After stepping from the shower, I slipped and grabbed hold of the shower curtain, ripping it off the rod and getting all twisted in it then falling to the ground and smacking my head. *I am not off to a good start today,* I thought, laying on the ground mangled up and rubbing my head. I just burst into laughter. I laughed so hard that my stomach hurt. And then, from nowhere, my laughter turned to tears. "Get a hold of yourself!" I snapped.

During my drive to work, I cranked the tunes. Music always calmed my nerves and relieved stress.

Thud, thud, thud.

Seriously! Why wouldn't it? Today of all days. I attacked the steering wheel with my fists of fury. *What else could go wrong?* But, in the midst of anger, I was thankful Dad had showed me how to change a tire.

I popped the truck and dug out the spare tire, jack, and lug wrench.

***

I arrived to work twenty minutes late, sweaty and needing a shower, probably reeking of body odor. I scurried into the bathroom and quickly closed the door behind me before anyone could see me.

Exhaling a big sigh, I leaned against the door and clenched my hands. I gripped a fistful of hair as I felt ready to rip it right out of my head and then released a dramatic silent scream. I shook my head as I stepped toward the mirror—mascara running, messy hair, black streaking from my cheekbone to my chin, and bloodshot eyes. I was a wreck. I needed to clean myself up before anyone saw me like this.

About five minutes had passed. I straightened my shirt and collar and took a gander in the mirror, approving my quick makeover and giving myself a fake smile to rally myself before I faced my staff. I cleared my throat and pulled open the door, ready to face the world.

"Good morning, Ms. Williams. It's so nice to see you. You have two patients waiting to see you. Anna has finished their cleanings." Monica was definitely a morning person.

I approached the dental rooms and turned around. "Monica, could you please make a run to Starbuck's and grab me my usual? With a flat tire, I didn't have time this morning."

Monica smiled. "Of course."

"Thank you. And while you're there, pick something up for yourself. And maybe grab a few muffins and bagels for the rest of the staff."

"Sounds good. I'll be back shortly."

My staff had been phenomenal. I needed to show my appreciation more. I decided I'd treat them to Happy Hour at a local pub someday.

"April, could you please watch the front desk? I sent Monica to Starbuck's."

"Yeah, of course." April motioned to a patient. "This is Mr. Stewart. This is his first time in a dentist office in twenty years. I just finished his cleaning, and his X-rays are hanging for your examination."

"Thank you, April."

"Mr. Stewart, twenty years is a long time."

"Twenty-three, actually," he replied nervously, stirring in the chair.

"Well, Mr. Stewart, you have quite a few cavities. Eleven, to be exact. You'll have to make a few appointments to get these filled. Looks like you may need a root canal. Are you experiencing any pain?"

"Sometimes. It comes and goes."

"If it gets any worse, please call the office, and we can get you in sooner to get it fixed. Why don't you go to the front desk, and April can schedule your next appointment? It was very nice meeting you, Mr. Stewart. Have a nice day." I smile, shaking his hand.

SEALED RECORDS
(TREVOR)

"I don't get it, Trevor. This case has everyone baffled, especially the police." Rachel turned her face away. "This case just doesn't add up. I'm losing tons of sleep trying to wrap my brain around this. It makes no sense." Rachel sighed, folding her arms.

"This stuff takes time, sweetheart. You can't rush it. A clue will come up eventually. It has to."

"I don't know … It's got everyone stumped. Fingerprints are all over the crime scenes, but no matches found in the database. There are no witnesses. The crime scenes are disorganized and sloppy, and they have nothing!" Rachel rubbed her forehead.

I grabbed the bottle of 2007 Nosotros and top off our wine glasses. "What about motive?" I raise the glass of wine, and the black-raspberry flavor rolls over my lips.

"That's the only thing we have going for us." Rachel pursed her lips. "I had a connection dig deep into each of the victims' pasts to shine any light on why someone would want them dead. And not just dead, but brutally murdered, mutilated, and tortured."

"And ...?" I lean in closer, raising my eyebrows.

"They all spent time in jail for heinous crimes." Rachel leaned back in her chair and drew a long breath.

"Makes perfect sense why someone would torture them."

Rachel shifted nervously in her chair and leaned in closer again, almost speaking in a whisper now. "They got away with a slap on the hand, spent hardly any time behind bars. They apparently know how to work the system. Maybe the killer is someone who works in the courthouse. Maybe the judge is corrupt and being paid off. Who knows? The system is broken. You don't know who you can trust anymore."

"Wow! And why hasn't this been made public?"

"Because the records are sealed, and the information is from an unreliable source, dismissed from law enforcement for misconduct. Knew a little too much information. No one likes a person who creates waves and holds people accountable. They were forced to resign."

"How long have you known this?" I asked nervously, shifting my eyes.

"A couple weeks." Rachel looked down and away.

"And you didn't tell me?" I sighed with disappointment.

"I'm telling you now."

"Why would you keep something like this from me?"

"Calm down. It's a sensitive case, Trevor. I can't just spill my guts about everything. I have to be careful who I tell."

I stood, clenched my jaw and flared my nose. I walked away from Rachel and slammed my fists on the counter. "Jesus Christ!"

Rachel flinched. "I'm sorry, babe."

"So, you're saying you don't trust me?"

"I didn't say that."

"Yes, you did," I snapped, cracking my knuckles.

"I'm sorry, Trevor. That's not what I meant."

"I thought we told each other ... everything."

"We do. But I think you've had a little too much to drink tonight, Trevor."

"Don't go there, Rachel."

"Come, sit down. Relax."

I paced back and forth, taking deep breaths and trying to calm myself before I said or did something I may later regret. "Rachel. I understand you don't feel comfortable sharing every detail about this case with me, but this is a huge breakthrough. A case with absolutely no leads, no conclusive evidence, and you find this out and have known about it for two weeks and it hasn't even come up in conversation?" I covered my face with my hands and shook my head. "It feels to me like you're hiding something or you don't trust me. And that hurts immensely, especially after everything we've been through."

"I'm sorry, Trevor." Rachel tapped the chair next to her. "Please sit down."

I was more upset with her comment about being careful who she talks to, but I needed to stop being so stubborn and talk this through. I refused to go to bed angry; it wasn't good for either of us. That's one thing Mary had taught me about relationships—never go to bed angry.

I slid out a chair and sat then turned my chair toward Rachel—no table between us, just two bodies facing each other, open and vulnerable.

Rachel grabbed my hands and looked at me. "Trevor, please don't be upset with me. I didn't mean for that to come out the way it did." Rachel sniffled. "I trust you completely, I really do. I probably wouldn't be as stressed if I just unloaded all the thoughts instead of suppressing them." Rachel sighed, shaking her leg. "Getting a hold of the records will be the hard part. You need security access. Everything is password-protected and high security. I need to find a criminal who knows how to hack their system."

"Breaking the law now, are we?"

"Well, I wouldn't be. Just paying someone to. It's for a good cause. Need to catch the killer before they do it again."

"How would you go about finding someone that could do that?"

"I'm not sure exactly."

"You ready for bed?" I stood, extending my hand.

As Rachel rose to her feet, I wrapped my arms around her and gave her a tight squeeze, holding her for a moment. "I'm sorry, baby, for getting upset with you and losing my temper. I don't like when we fight." I released my grip and looked Rachel in the eyes with a half-smile. I whispered into her ear, "All this breaking the law talk is making me horny. Want to play out a scenario?" I flitted my eyebrows up and down.

"Like what?"

"I pull you over for speeding, and you plead with me not to give you a ticket, and just improvise from there." I slapped her firm ass with an ear-to-ear grin.

Rachel yelped as her face flushed with color, and she giggled playfully. Grabbing my face, she seductively kissed my lips and grabbed my hand, leading me to the bedroom. "Don't forget the handcuffs."

***

I quickly glanced behind me, breathing heavy. My legs burned from running so fast and the adrenaline pumping through my veins. I tripped on an overgrown root and cracked my knee on the forest ground. The pain radiated through my leg as I shrieked.

I clasped my mouth, eyes darting frantically. I stumbled to my feet. Sharp rocks and dry leaves crunched under my mangled bare feet, leaving a trail of warm blood behind me. My heart pounded so hard that I heard it echoing in my skull.

I had to stop, take a break for just a moment to catch my breath. My throat felt dry and scratchy from gasping for air. I frantically looked around; my eyes widened with fear. The darkness played tricks on me. A shadow darted behind a nearby tree, startling me. I gasped then held my breath as I fought the impulse to turn around. My heart pounded fiercely; my hands were clenched into a fist, ready to attack my predator. Fear tortured my thoughts. My stomach twisted into a violent cramp.

A loud crash paralyzed my soul. I tried to run, but my legs felt heavy, making it nearly impossible. The shadow darted from behind the tree, charging at me with a machete.

I bellowed a curdling scream and awoke from a sound sleep, drenched in a fear-induced sweat.

BLUE RIDGE MURDER
(TREVOR)

Another murder. Four now in six months. This one was in Blue Ridge. Everyone panicked. I'd seen several moving trucks within the last couple weeks. People were scared and moving far away, I assumed. No one felt safe anymore. The police had no leads or suspects, which made it even more horrifying. Whomever committed these murders got away with them, and, until law enforcement catches them, there could be more.

A newspaper article last week reported the sale of guns had risen 300% this year. Fear had induced towns within a two-hundred-mile radius, and the town of Blue Ridge implemented a dusk-to-dawn curfew.

A tragic accident occurred a few days ago. Someone had shot an innocent man. A family had lost a father and husband. The victim had parked in a nearby neighborhood during his family vacation to knock on someone's door to ask directions. The paranoid homeowner didn't recognize the man, and, when he opened the door, he shot the driver in the head, killing him instantly.

***

The authorities finally released the details of the murders to the public after much uproar and protests. The public demanded details, stating they had every right to know, so they could protect their families. Keeping the details a secret made matters worse and everyone more paranoid.

My smart, sexy wife dug up the dirt on the victims' sealed cases. She should have been an FBI criminal investigator instead of working as an investigative journalist for the local newspaper, but she enjoyed her job. She loved being the brains at the *Redwood Times*. She got satisfaction when she would unearth information before the police could. She had an eye and some connections she wouldn't name. Top secret stuff. She's always saying, *"If I tell you, I'll have to kill you."* She always tried to look dreadfully serious, but she couldn't keep a straight face for long. She always cracked. She was incredibly cute when she did it too. Reminded me why I fell in love with her. She had such a sweet, kind spirit. And of course, she tolerated my shit; I could be a moody SOB at times.

"Trevor, I've been practicing my speech for the detectives for days now and hoped you'd sit down and just listen without saying a word or interrupting, and let me know if what I have is too much or not enough or if I should change anything."

"Yeah, of course, sweetheart." I sat in the oversized leather recliner and listened intently.

"First murder victim was fifty-four-year-old Steven Howard of Roanoke, who only served nine months in county jail for sexually molesting little boys. The killer tattooed the number nine on his left buttocks. The second murder was forty-three-year-old Robert Belview of Charlottesville. He burglarized elderly people, and they charged him with multiple felonies. He was released after serving just six months in prison. The killer tattooed the number six on his forearm. He stole millions of dollars over seventeen years. The police never found all the money. They confiscated his house, vacation homes, cars, boats, motorhome, guns—anything worth value—for restitution, but it barely scratched the surface. One of his victims was found dead in his home after hanging himself. Such a tragedy. The third murder was forty-nine-year-old Daniel Balaton of Richmond. He was charged with embezzlement. He spent just three months in jail. The killer tattooed the number three on the side of his neck. He embezzled millions of dollars over his twenty-two-year tenure as general manager of several grain and feed elevators. As a result of his embezzlement, the company went bankrupt, affecting all the farmers, employees, suppliers, and vendors." Rachel took a deep breath then sighed with disappointment. "As for the forth murder, it just happened so, unfortunately, we have no details.

"I learned in my research that three types of serial killers exist: the medical killer, the organized killer, and the disorganized killer. Although the medical killer is very rare, people have become involved in the medical industry to facilitate their crimes with the perfect cover. If it appears the victim has died a natural death, there's no reason to suspect foul play. The organized killer is the most difficult to identify and apprehend. They are usually highly intelligent and very meticulous. They plan every detail of the crime in advance, and they leave no incriminating evidence behind. The disorganized killer rarely plans their victims' deaths. They usually strike at random whenever an opportunity arises. And, in most cases, the victims are just in the wrong place at the wrong time. Disorganized killers take no precautions to cover their crimes and tend to move to different towns or states regularly to avoid capture. They usually have low IQs and are extremely antisocial. They rarely have close friends or family and do not stay in one place for too long." Rachel paced.

"With that being said, it also looks like we have two types of serial killers on our hands: organized and disorganized. Even though the crime scenes seem disorganized and sloppy, we have no witnesses and no incriminating evidence, and, even though we have fingerprints, none of them are in our database. Each crime was in a different town. Each murder victim had been charged with a felony, and each murder victim was tattooed with a number. We have deciphered that the number resembles the months they had spent incarcerated. Any questions?" Rachel exhaled a big sigh and plopped onto the couch.

I smiled. "Rachel, that was fantastic. But, just between us, do you think whoever is committing these murders might be doing society a favor? A vigilante maybe?"

Rachel nodded. "The thought has crossed my mind."

"This serial killer is taking the lives of bad people, not innocent. These so-called murder victims ruined the lives of many, and the system obviously failed miserably, showing the real victims here no mercy."

"This is true. Life can be cruel sometimes." Rachel lowered her head.

"You always hope that if the system fails, karma will bite a big chunk from their ass. Maybe this vigilante *is* their karma, if you believe in karma."

"I do. I'm a true believer that everything happens for a reason. Karma could definitely play a major role in that."

"Cause and effect. I believe every action and intent influences your future. Karma is simply getting what you give or reaping what you sow. But there's good and bad karma."

"I agree completely. Every action, every thought brings about its own corresponding consequence."

"And, according to laws of nature, one must pay for all their actions. Do you think karma is blind chance, pure accident, or do we get what we deserve?"

"Some people may think it could be a little bit of each, but I don't believe things happen coincidently. I'm a firm believer that everything happens for a reason, whether we understand it at the time or not."

"I get where you're coming from, but do you truly believe that the victims of the murder victims—let's say, for instance, the little boys who Stephen Howard raped—that it happened to them for a reason? Did they deserve it? Or are there things we just don't understand? Or maybe some people are so corrupt and evil that they defy the laws of nature?"

"Maybe someone close to them is being punished."

"Why not punish them?"

"Maybe the only way to make them suffer is to hurt or take away someone they love. Some people could care less if you hurt them. They have the attitude of *do whatever you want to me, but, if you lay a finger on so-and-so, you'll pay the price.*"

"I get that. I see where you're coming from. But you still don't have me convinced."

"What don't you understand? Everything happens for a reason, Trevor. Everything!"

GIRLS
NIGHT OUT
(BELLA)

I walked onto my porch, sat my coffee on the end table, and climbed into my red hanging hammock lounger to peacefully admire the sunrise. It was my favorite seat to read in and, of course, watch the sunrise. I had the same chair on my back patio to enjoy the sunset, except that chair was blue.

A slight breeze caressed my skin as the leaves rustled in the wind, carrying the tantalizing aroma that perfectly captures the calming scent of lilacs and lavender. Studies proved that lavender slowed the heartbeat, relaxed muscles, and reduced stress, as for the reason I had a lavender oil diffuser in my bedroom when I slept. At times like these, it was essential. My anxiety and stress had been through the roof. A night out in town might be in order, to let loose and have some fun. I acted so serious all the time. I needed to defuse before I went bananas. But who should I call?

My only friend had moved across country, and I hadn't seen her in years. But who was I kidding? She hated me; she wanted nothing to do with me. The girls at the office were always an option. I'd meant to treat them to Happy Hour, with plenty of drinks and appetizers. My favorite was the sampler, with quesadillas, potato skins, mozzarella sticks, and boneless buffalo wings. Just thinking about it made me hungry.

I took a sip of coffee, burning my lips. I laid back and enjoyed the lovely view while I finished my cup of coffee. I meandered to the kitchen and threw together a nice breakfast with two fried eggs over-medium, two slices of crispy bacon, hash browns, and a slice of toast with homemade raspberry jam.

Sitting alone at the table in silence made me feel sad and lonely. I was twenty-three years old; I should be partying and going out to the bar every night. Or settling down in a relationship and talking about having a baby. But, instead, I have a boring life—the same daily routine: go to work, come home to an empty house, and read in my little nook. I don't hang out with friends. I don't date. I don't go to bars. I'm pathetic.

I stood from my tiny kitchen table and brushed the crumbs from my plate into the trash. Being the clean freak that I am, I refused to let dirty dishes sit in the sink. I turned the faucet and filled the sink with the dirty dishes from breakfast.

As much as I enjoyed my time alone, I sometimes wondered what it felt like to wake up every morning next to someone. I gazed out the window, daydreaming. I wondered what it would be like to cook for someone, to have meaningful conversations with, to tease and laugh at each other, that special someone to vent to and have a shoulder to cry on—a best friend and a lover.

I shrieked. Water splashed onto the floor and all over the front of me. I quickly turned off the faucet and drained some water. I shook my head, trying to clear the ridiculous thoughts. I was a loner, always had been, always will be. No use daydreaming and thinking my life would be any different. It was useless.

I enjoyed my time alone. I didn't answer to anyone but me. And better yet, I didn't have to listen to someone complain that I read too much and needed to spend more time with them. Maybe, if I was happy, I wouldn't escape into the depths of these pages and fantasize about an alternate existence, but the reality was, I loved reading.

My mind wandered with disappointment as I pondered the widespread access to videogames and screen time and fewer bookstores nowadays. Reading appealed less to children today, and some might have a negative stereotype of bookworms—a socially isolated loner sitting in a corner and reading while everyone played. I believed people who read a lot were intelligent, and it proved a great way to exercise the brain. Readers constantly followed plots and used vivid imagination. I also believed readers understood empathy by interpreting feelings, emotions, and the mental state of others. Reading could also improve memory. Reading and getting lost in a book held big cognitive benefits. And besides all the other benefits, I thought, most importantly, reading might be a great way to prevent Alzheimer's disease. But why was I defending my reading habits or love for books? I had no one to answer to but me. If I ever have a child, I'd introduce them to the lovely world of books and the benefits of reading on our brain.

***

After a long ten-hour day and endless appointments, it was finally time to enjoy a night out with my staff to show my appreciation for all their hard work these past few months. I hadn't anticipated how much business our teeth cleaning promotions would garner. The office was like a revolving door and was great for business and had most definitely built our clientele base. I learned it was all about having reasonable prices and not getting greedy. I still had a business to run, but making a ton of money was not my priority. I pay my staff well, and I still make good money.

We laughed and had a good time, but I hadn't eaten much and felt a bit tipsy. I wasn't about to lose my staff's respect, so I switched to water and ordered another appetizer sampler to share.

I noticed an older gentleman sitting at a table by himself in the corner. He kept glancing in our direction. I tried not to pay much attention, but something didn't feel right. He gave me the creeps. He was a tall, thin man with beady eyes and greasy hair, probably in his mid-fifties. His clothes were dirty and ratty, like he had worn them for years. He sat with an empty glass, glaring at me. I tried ignoring him, but his glares made me uneasy. I didn't even want to make eye contact with him.

"Is everything okay, Isabella?" Monica asked.

"Yeah, I'm fine." I shot her a fake smile, trying to hide my nerves. I approached the bar. "Could I please have a shot of Crown Royal apple?" I desperately needed something to help calm my nerves. Not sure if it would help, but it was worth a try.

The bartender grabbed a shot glass from under the bar and placed it on the counter then reached for the bottle behind him on the glass shelving against a long mirror. My nerves were written all over my face. No wonder Monica had asked if everything was okay. I raised my hands, covering my face, rubbing my eyebrows outward and down my cheeks, and stopping at my chin. I took a deep breath and exhaled.

The bartender finished pouring the shot, and I raised the glass to my lips and quickly tipped back my head and slammed the shot glass onto the counter. The liquor had a slightly tart, crisp-apple flavor, with notes of caramel and light spice, ending with a smooth finish of refined apple notes—just what I needed. The slight burn stretching from my lips down my throat was delightful as I licked my lips. I closed my eyes as my nerves subsided almost immediately.

I glanced in the corner of my eye and noticed the grungy gentleman no longer sat at the table. I sighed with relief and returned to the table.

"Is everything okay, Isabella?" Erica asked.

"Yeah, of course." I smiled. "Did anyone see if the gentleman sitting over at that table left?" I pointed toward the table.

"What gentleman?" Sadie asked, scanning the bar.

"He was sitting right over there. He was dirty, had greasy hair and old grungy clothes."

"I didn't realize you were into those type of guys." Sarah chuckled.

"No, no, no!" I rolled my eyes. "He just gave me the creeps. Kept looking over and staring at us, me in particular. Made me feel uneasy."

"So that's what was bothering you," Allison said, slapping her forehead. "I never saw the guy. Did any of you?"

"No," everyone replied, shaking their heads.

Something wasn't right. How did no one see him except me? I approached the bartender. "Did the gentleman sitting at that table leave for the night?" I pointed at the empty table.

"No one sat there all night, ma'am."

"Are you sure?"

"Yeah, positive."

"Okay, thanks."

"So, what did the bartender say?"

"No one has been there all night." I shrugged. "I must be going crazy."

***

Finally home, I flipped on the switch, closed the door behind me, leaned back against the door and sighed. *I swear I saw a man at that table staring at me. I'm not making it up, and I'm not going crazy. Or am I?* I covered my face with my hands and took a deep breath.

I dropped my hands and saw the man from the bar standing on the opposite side of the room.

A machete protruded from his skull, blood streaming down his face. His wide and unblinking eyes bore into me.

I rubbed my eyes. He slowly raised his hand, pointing at me. I stood motionless, fear-stricken.

His arm remained extended, pointing at me, while a deep red puddle formed at his feet.

BANG!

Startled, I gasped. I whipped my head toward the sound. I quickly looked back at the man, but he was gone—vanished into thin air.

THE
BREAK-IN
(BELLA)

I hadn't slept much in weeks. The man in my house had totally freaked me out. I still see him—machete, blood and all—every time I closed my eyes. He haunted my every thought, haunted my dreams. What did he want? What was he telling me, and why could I only see him? I didn't believe in ghosts, but I didn't know how else to explain it. Unless it was just my mind playing tricks on me.

I shook my head, vanquishing the disturbing image. I passed a mirror and stopped. My eyes looked tired—a ring of darkness around them, skin pale. I looked awful. At times like this, I wished I had sleeping pills. I'd ruled out therapists; they were all just a bunch of frauds. They pretended to know, but they have no clue. My only option was to buy something over-the-counter. I was desperate—maybe NyQuil?

Dr. Marshall came to mind. I hadn't thought about him in months. That asshole had kicked me out of his office with no explanation. This no sleep thing allowed me to think more. I wondered if he had kept the recording from my last visit or if he had destroyed it. The only way I could be sure was to sneak in after closing. I needed to know what had been said. It must have been serious enough that he didn't want to see me anymore. I must figure out a way to break-in. I didn't want to just wing it and get caught, so I needed to really think this one through before I made a mistake I would regret.

Getting caught would open a can of worms. I needed to be smart about this.

***

The moon shone brightly against the blanket of darkness, casting shadows and an eerie silence. My footsteps echoed with every step. Crickets chirped in the distance. I had always preferred nighttime over the day—quiet and peaceful. The city slept at night, while daytime lured crowds, traffic, and lots of noise. I understood why Mary had loved small-town living. This time of night was the only glimpse of stillness I got.

Wearing only a thin jacket, I shuddered from the cool breeze and quickened my pace to keep warm. The glow from streetlamps and traffic lights illuminated my way. Only a few blocks remained.

Footsteps sounded behind me. I gasped, eyes widened as I halted and slowly turned my head—but nothing was there. I continued to walk slowly with caution, glancing back every few steps. Nothing. Maybe I had imagined it; the night tended to play tricks on loners who traveled with nothing but their thoughts.

"Isabella," a voice whispered.

I whipped around quickly. My gaze darted frantically in the darkness. It had sounded like the whisper had come from right behind me.

"Who's there?" I hollered, scared.

"Go home," it whispered louder.

"What do you want?"

"Go home," the voice repeated.

"Why? I need to do this. I need to know." A sudden feeling of dread overwhelmed my soul. My chest and stomach twisted and turned into knots.

Someone was warning me. Would something bad happen? Or would the file reveal something better left unknown? I second-guessed my decision to burglarize Dr. Marshall's office. Would the unknown haunt my thoughts forever, or would the evidence I might uncover haunt me? Regardless, no matter what I decided, one would haunt me.

I needed to tread carefully. The voice was warning me; maybe I should listen. Or maybe the voice was just a figment of my sleep-deprived imagination. I played a tug-o-war with my thoughts. To do, or not to do? That was the real question.

I *needed* to know, regardless what I might discover. The anxiety overwhelmed me. I inhaled a deep breath and approached the main building door. I pulled the bobby pins from my jacket pocket and picked the lock. I looked behind me in both directions, making sure I was alone and no one was watching. I felt it unlock, and I pushed open the door and reached for my pocket flashlight.

I better be quick. A silent alarm may have already alerted the police. I bounded the stairs to the third floor. I wasn't about to wait for the slow elevator I had ridden so many times when I was crippled.

I approached Dr. Marshall's office and turned the doorknob. Locked. "Dammit!" I grabbed for the bobby pins again. My heart pounded in my chest; my hands shook, and I panted from running up two flights of stairs. I stuck the flashlight in my mouth, so I could see the lock better, and I dropped the bobby pins. My nerves got the best of me. Stumbling around, I felt for the pins on the floor.

"You don't have time for mistakes. Pull yourself together, Isabella," I said aloud.

I found the pins and tried again, holding my breath this time. I finally unlocked the door. I ran to the filing cabinet in the corner and pulled on the handle with no luck. "It's locked too!" I let out a frustrated sigh.

I fumbled to unlock the filing cabinet but, with luck, got it immediately. I slid open the drawer, rummaging through the alphabetical files. Of course, mine started with *W* and was not in this drawer; it only went up to *L*. I crouched to the bottom drawer and unlocked it within seconds.

I better find it fast and get out of here before the police barge in and charge me with breaking and entering—a felony in the state of Virginia.

I yanked the handle, and it squealed loudly as the wheels gave resistance.

Something was behind me. I gasped, spun and shone the light around the room. I noticed moving feet on the couch behind Dr. Marshall's desk. My eyes widened with fear. I turned back around and fumbled quickly through the files.

Found it. Isabella Williams. I grabbed it, eased the cabinet shut and stood. I turned around and yelped.

Dr. Marshall stood right in front of me, rubbing his eyes. "What are you doing here, Isabella?"

I turned to flee, but he gripped my bicep.

"I can't let you leave with that." He ripped the file from my hands.

I clocked him square in the nose. His bone cracked under my knuckles, and warm liquid ran down my wrist.

He screamed, dropping the file as the papers scattered across the floor.

"I'm so sorry. I didn't want to hurt you, but I *need* these."

I gathered the papers together quickly. I stood, looked at Dr. Marshall holding his nose in pain and ran out the door. I tripped down the stairs and rolled to the bottom. I clenched the folder to not lose any papers as I hit my head on the tile floor. I grunted and rubbed my head. I stumbled to my feet, trying to regain balance.

I ran down the next flight of stairs and out the front door not looking back, sprinting as fast as I could.

THE VISIT
(BELLA)

It had been five days, and the police and Dr. Marshall had not called or knocked on my door. Maybe since I had stolen my own file, Dr. Marshall decided not to press charges.

I looked through my file, but, of course, I found no tape recording of our last visit nor any useful information. The last page stated that after the hypnotherapy, Dr. Marshall decided it was in his best interest to not see me anymore for personal reasons, due to information he had learned in our session. But, of course, he listed no explanation. It also stated that, in his professional opinion, I had symptoms of dissociative identity disorder. I wasn't exactly sure what that means. The files also stated that I lost time and didn't remember anything that happened during these times and why he felt it necessary to use hypnotherapy.

Stealing the file had not answered any of my questions. I needed to find that tape. And why would Dr. Marshall sleep at his office and not at home? Maybe he fought with his girlfriend, and he had decided to go to his office, which made the most logical sense, but I felt bad for breaking his nose, nonetheless. But I hadn't expected him to be at his office after hours. If he hadn't been there, I would have never hit him. I had been desperate; I needed that file.

I glanced at my phone—four missed calls from Dad and he had left a voicemail. I checked my voicemail. "Isabella, you need to call me as soon as you get this message. It's urgent." *Click.*

His tone concerned me, so I called him right back. "Hey, Dad. You called?"

"Bella, have you watched the news lately?"

"No. I haven't turned on the TV in days. Why? What's going on?"

"They found your old therapist, Dr. Marshall, dead in his office four days ago."

"*What?*"

"The police are going through all his patient files and asked his secretary if anyone would have been upset with him or have any reason to want to hurt him. Rachel said the secretary mentioned your name. Is there anything we should know?"

"Why would my name come up?"

"The secretary said, at your last session, you stormed from the office and never came back. Out of all the patient files, yours is the only one missing."

"At our last session, Dr. Marshall hypnotized me to get inside my head. He said hypnotherapy might reveal things I have subconsciously hidden. After the session, he told me he wouldn't be able to see me anymore and told me not to come back."

"Any explanation?"

"No. That was the strangest part. He refused to tell me what I had said. But whatever it was, he was so upset that he didn't want to see me anymore."

"That's weird. Just going to give you a heads up, Isabella. The police will be stopping by to ask you questions."

"Okay. Thanks, Dad."

"Be safe, Bella. I love you."

"I love you too, Dad."

Click.

***

Oh, my God! My fingerprints. I gasped. But I had a legitimate excuse. I needed my file. They might think that was the motive. What do I say? What do I do?

Knock, knock knock.

Just be honest. They must believe me. I didn't do anything wrong here—except commit a felony. I had broken into a building and had stolen something. Granted, it was information on *me*, but, if I had been meant to have it, it would've already been in my possession, not locked in someone else's filing cabinet. This wasn't good. This was *not* good.

Knock! Knock! Knock!

"Hold on! I'm coming," I hollered from the other room. I closed my eyes, took a deep breath and opened the door, smiling.

"Ms. William?" A husky man stood in front of me.

I quickly surveyed his police uniform, neatly trimmed mustache, dark combed-back hair, and brown deep-set eyes. I focused on his wide mouth adorned with big, white straight teeth—picture perfect, like a dental advertisement. I cocked my head, wondering if I was the only person who obsessed about teeth.

"Ms. Williams?" the officer repeated.

I noticed the gentleman standing next to him—tall and slender with a serious expression, his arms crossed and his eyebrows tight—glaring at me.

"Yes?"

"Could you please come with us to the station?"

"What for?"

"We just have a few questions to ask you about your psychiatrist, Dr. Joseph Marshall."

"Why can't you just ask me right here? Did something happen to him?"

"It's best if we do this at the police station."

"Am I being arrested?"

"No. Just have a few questions to ask you."

"What about?"

"Just follow us. It'll be much easier if you cooperate."

"Fine. Let me grab my purse."

***

After two long hours of interviewing, the police told me to go home. But they highly suggested for me not to leave town or travel anytime soon. They remained tight-lipped about the murder details.

Another murder—that was five now. No wonder moving trucks appeared in droves in the area.

I couldn't believe I didn't feel a tad bit sorry about Dr. Marshall's murder. I'd think I'd be a little upset. But what was important to me was finding the tape of our session. I wondered if the police had it. If they did, they hadn't mentioned it to me, and I wasn't about to ask.

Ring … Ring … Ring …

"Hey, Dad. I just got out of a two-hour meeting with the police. Are you home?"

"No, honey. I'm at the jobsite, but I should be off work by five, if you want to come over and have dinner with me and Rachel. We'd love your company."

"Sounds good. Can I bring anything?"

"Just yourself."

"Okay, Dad. See you later. Bye."
Click.

***

"Wow, it smells amazing! What's on tonight's menu?" I asked, deeply inhaling the aromas.

"I tried a new recipe. It's a parmesan-crusted chicken with bacon cream sauce, twice-baked potato, and oven-roasted broccoli," Rachel replied, licking her fingers. "Your father stepped into the other room. He had to grab something for me. He should be back shortly." Rachel smiled. "So, I heard the police paid you a visit."

"Yeah. They brought me to the station to ask me some questions. Just routine." I shifted my weight.

"Why you?" Rachel opened the oven door, inspecting the food.

"I was his former patient. His secretary told the police that I had left on bad terms, and my file was the only one missing from his office."

"Left on bad terms?"

"Yeah. We had a hypnotherapy session. He said it might help with the suppressed memories. After the session, he was very upset. He said he didn't want to see me anymore and wouldn't explain why."

"That's odd," Rachel replied with a puzzled expression.

"That's what I thought. I haven't slept well. I've been obsessing about what I said in the session that had upset him so much." I pulled out a chair and sat. "So, I decided a few nights ago to break into his office and steal my file, hoping it would give me some answers." I looked at my hands. "But when I broke in, he was sleeping on the couch in his office." I sighed. "He woke up and tried taking the file from me, but I desperately needed to know. So, I decked him in the nose. I'm pretty sure I broke it. I felt his bones crunch, and it bled pretty badly. I took off running." I looked up, uncomfortably waiting for a response. "I swear, I didn't kill him. But I was probably the last person to see him alive, and my fingerprints are all over his office."

"Did you tell this to the police?"

"No. They'd think I was guilty, that-that I had killed him."

"Lying will make you look guilty, Isabella. Your story seems legit. Why lie about it?"

"Because he's ... *dead*!"

"*Ahem.*"

I turned to see Dad approach us. "How long have you been standing there?"

"Long enough to hear the whole story." He raised his eyebrows and sat in the chair next to me. "How have you been, sweetheart?" He placed his hand upon mine.

I gave him a half-smile. "Okay, I guess."

"Sorry to hear about your therapist."

"It's okay. I hadn't seen him in a long time."

"Did you find what you were looking for in your file?"

I sighed. "No."

"What exactly *were* you looking for?"

"A tape of our hypnotherapy session."

"It wasn't in there?"

"No."

"*Hm ...*"

"I have to go back. I have to find it."

"I'm sure the police scoured his office with a fine-tooth comb. For all you know, they have it."

"That's possible. But I wasn't about to ask them. That would make me look suspicious."

"Why are you so concerned about this tape? Can't you just let it go?"

"No. It's been bothering me. I can't sleep. I can't concentrate. It's driving me crazy."

"I can go by his office," Rachel interrupted. "I have a good eye. If the police don't have it and they overlooked it, I could find it." Rachel smiled, grabbing plates from the cabinet.

"She's right, Isabella. She has a gift. She should've been a private investigator."

"I work for the newspaper. They won't suspect anything." Rachel set the plates in front of us. "They'll just think I'm just digging up dirt for the office." She smiled.

"When do you think you'll stop by there?" I asked.

"Tonight."

***

Pacing neurotically, I checked the time. Rachel had been gone for over an hour now. I had told her that I would drive, but she insisted I stayed home—said she didn't want me to be an accessory if she got caught.

SLAM!

I ran to the window and pulled back the curtain. The porch light illuminated the driveway and cast eerie shadows in the night. A full moon hung low in the sky, bright and full of mystery. I'd always been fascinated by the night and outer space—the moon, stars, and planets, even aliens.

I approached the front door as it opened. "I started to worry. You were gone for over an hour. Did you find it?"

Rachel rummaged through her pockets. "I was about to give up and leave when something caught my attention." Rachel put out her hand, palm up.

"What is that?" I asked, squinting.

"It's a micro SD card." Rachel held it between her fingers, examining it. "Maybe it fell out of Isabella's file when she left that night."

"Where did you find it?"

 "In the corner of a stair."

"How in the world did you see it? That thing is so tiny."

She smirked. "I have a good eye."

"Apparently …" I nodded. "Do you think it could be the video of her session?"

"Only way to find out is to watch it."

"Not without Isabella."

"Why not?"

"Haven't you heard of doctor-patient confidentiality?"

"I don't care. This is an open murder investigation."

I rolled my eyes. "Do you have no boundaries?"

"Not when it comes to murder."

"It's Isabella. Come on, seriously? She has nothing to do with the murder."

"The police questioned her. She might be a suspect."

"We're talking about Isabella. She wouldn't hurt a fly."

"You heard her yourself. She broke his nose."

"He startled her. She didn't know he was sleeping in his office. Most people sleep at home."

"Are you making excuses for her?"

I shook my head. "No."

"Definitely sounds like it to me." Rachel raised her eyebrows and gave me a look. "What's so important about this session anyway?"

"The therapist refused to see her again after the visit, with no explanation."

"Isn't that a red flag? She broke into his office to steal it, remember? That's a felony."

"She's desperate to know what she had said under hypnosis. Wouldn't you be?"

"Maybe."

"Do you blame her?"

"Not really."

"Okay, then."

"Let's give it to Isabella, and if she wants us to see it, then we can."

"Aren't you a little curious?" Rachel sighed, folding her arms. "What if she never tells us?"

"That's her business. She's not a child. We'll call her in the morning and give it to her then."

"Fine, but I think you're making a big mistake."

"I won't go behind my daughter's back and watch a video of her therapy session without her permission. It feels wrong."

"She was the last person to see him alive. You don't find that a little disturbing?"

"It's just a coincidence."

"Maybe it is. But maybe it isn't."

THE
NIGHTMARES
CONTINUE
(TREVOR)

I glanced behind me, breathing heavy, my legs burning from sprinting, adrenaline pumping through my veins. I tripped and fell, twisting my knee as I screamed. The pain radiating through my leg was excruciating.

I tried to stand, but my legs collapsed. My heart pounded so hard that I heard it echoing in my skull. I dragged myself behind a huge oak tree to hide. I peeked around the trunk; my eyes widened with fear.

The darkness played tricks on me as a shadow darted from behind a nearby tree. I startled, quickly clasping my mouth. My heart pounded fiercely as fear tortured my thoughts, my stomach twisting into a violent cramp. A loud crash paralyzed me. I closed my eyes tight, hoping whatever was hunting me disappears. I couldn't bare the urge to look anymore.

I slowly peeked around the trunk again, and the shadow charged at me with a machete. I let out a curdling scream. I couldn't run. I couldn't hide. I just closed my eyes and prayed that I'd awaken from this terrible nightmare. But, when I opened my eyes, I was still in the forest paralyzed by fear.

The sound of dry leaves and crunching sticks got closer and closer. I summoned the courage to look again, my body trembling. It was Isabella sporting a crazed look in her eyes, staring at me and holding a machete dripping with blood. A drop hit my hair-raised arm as it dissolved my skin and shredded the meat and bones, but I felt nothing. The ground underneath me caved, and I freefell into a hole of darkness.

My eyes flung open. I lay in bed, safe with Rachel sound asleep next to me.

I lay in bed for a while but couldn't fall back to sleep. My thoughts ran rampant. All these years, I'd had the same recurring nightmare, but it changed just a tad each time. The last few had changed drastically. And now, Isabella had appeared in my nightmare, holding a machete. Bizarre. I'd heard that thoughts and pre-bedtime discussions could insert themselves into dreams, and that was probably what had happened. We had debated about Isabella, and now Isabella had a role in my recurring nightmare.

I quietly slid from the bed, trying not to wake my sleeping beauty. I slipped on my white robe hanging on the closet door. My feet felt cold against the marble floors as I traversed the hallway to the kitchen.

I poured a tall glass of orange juice as I gazed at my reflection in the window, staring blankly. The cold liquid dripped down my hand and snapped me back into reality. I grabbed a paper towel and cleaned the spill on the counter and washed my hands. I stood still, lost in thought. Parched, I raised the glass to my dry lips and gulped every refreshing drop in just seconds then wiped my lips with the back of my hand.

The old grandfather clock chimed the top of the hour, disturbing the silence. *What time is it?* I rubbed my eyes and yawned. Two o'clock. I had bought the beautiful clock at an antique shop downtown. Standing at approximately seventy-seven inches tall, it was made of dark walnut and carved with stunning accents and a gold-plated face and pendulum. I'd always loved antiques. They brought character and wisdom to our complicated world. My favorite had always been the grandfather clock; the close second was the antique wall-mounted telephone in the study, also made of dark walnut.

My mind wandered easily. I dragged my feet to the living room and collapsed on the leather couch. I grabbed the book I'd been reading—a short-story collection called *Different Seasons* by Stephen King. I ran my fingers along the pages where I'd placed my bookmark and read "Rita Hayworth and Shawshank Redemption."

***

My eyes had grown heavy and became hard to keep open. They slowly fluttered, drifting in and out of sleep, slipping deeper into dreamland.

I walked down a dark deserted gravel road in the middle of nowhere, trees arching over and extending their branches into what resembles a never-ending tunnel. All I heard was the wind howling as the moon illuminated my way. The stars sprayed the sky with thousands of glitter specks.

A dark figure stood at the end of the road. I squinted to get a better look. *Who is that?* I quickened my pace. The tunnel of trees stretched forever. The faster I ran, the farther away I seemed to be, as if I walked backward. Confused, I stopped as everything around me spun. Dizzy, I leaned against the tree to catch my balance.

"*Treeevooor,*" the voice echoed.

I looked around, but I saw no one.

"*Treeevooor.*"

"Who's there?" My gaze darted frantically in the dark.

The trees on either side of me extended their branches toward me like long skeleton fingers, wrapping them gently around my feet and ankles and up my legs as another grabbed hold of my arms and around my torso and chest then squeezed tighter and tighter, making it hard to breathe. I tried to scream, but nothing escaped my trembling lips. It squeezed so tight that I felt my bones crush under its massive grip. My windpipe crushed. I panicked as I desperately gasped for air. I felt lightheaded as everything around me faded.

My life flashed before my eyes—images of my mom laying passed out, covered in vomit, and a glass of alcohol tipped over on the table; sitting across the table from my dad at breakfast when I was a kid; the beach; the first day I met Julia; Julia lying unconscious in a coma; the arbor that comes crashing down during our wedding; the first time I laid eyes on my baby girl; the look in Julia's eyes, dead; a door opening as Mary's face appears; my parents happy, kissing; the dead bunny; the fire; Isabella slamming a door in my face; Rachel's contagious laughter; Mary, dead; Isabella holding a machete.

I gasped, and my eyes flung open, heart pounding, as I realized I lay on the couch with a book in my lap. Relieved, I inhaled a deep breath. The dream had felt so real that it terrified me.

The sound of shattering glass from the other room startled me. I rose, stumbling to my feet. Scanning the room, I noticed a picture on the floor. I gently picked it up and flipped it over. Our family picture, shattered.

How did this fall over? Confused, I picked up the pieces.

SECRETS
(BELLA)

I felt depressed and lonely, and I missed Mary. I hadn't visited the guesthouse since she had passed. I told Dad I'd stop by this weekend to sort through her belongings, see what I wanted to keep before he and Rachel emptied the place. I think he had a hard time dealing with her death too.

I wondered if her spirit lingered in the house. Spirits sometimes get attached to their belongings if they didn't pass to the other side, trapped on Earth with unfinished business. But Mary had passed peacefully in her sleep. I could see no reason she would be trapped in-between. Feeling her presence would comfort me. I missed her dearly.

I stood on the front porch with my hand on the doorknob, hesitating. *What am I waiting for?* I turned the knob and pushed through the door.

The house looked clean, like I had remembered, before Mary had turned for the worse—calling me Natalie, wandering off, getting lost and not finding her way back home, not getting up to watch the sunrise, like she always loved to do, and, of course, not keeping her place clean and tidy. The smell of bleach hung in the air. Dad had paid

Mary's home nurse to clean the place from top to bottom one last time after she had passed. The idea of her dying in the house had disturbed him.

A layer of dust had settled on some of her belongings. I ran my finger along the living room's entertainment center, leaving a trace from one edge to the other then wiping the dust on my pants. I walked to her bedroom and stopped in the entryway. An overwhelming feeling of dread overcame me. My throat tightened, making it hard to swallow. The room was dark and gloomy, and I swore the temperature dropped about ten degrees. I wrapped my arms around myself and rubbed them, trying to keep warm. My gaze wandering around the room. *Where to start?*

I got on my hands and knees and looked under the bed. Other than a few dust bunnies, nothing was under there. I sat on the floor, legs crossed and deep in thought. It saddened me as I pondered what I really knew about Mary's life before she had come to live with us.

Mary had been very secretive when it came to her life before us. She didn't like discussing it; it caused her much pain. I respected her wishes and never pried. All I know was that she had lost both her parents in a tragic car accident when she was just twelve years old; she had attended South Dakota State University to become a nurse, just like her mother; she had married Elliott, and they'd had a daughter, Natalie—Dad's biological mother; her husband had died—but she never explained how, it had been a very touchy subject, and I never pushed the issue. I also know that her daughter had died in a car accident after Dad was born.

What I never understood was why Mary didn't raise Dad. He had been put up for adoption and never learned about her until I was five years old and diagnosed with cardiomyopathy. He had his adoption unsealed to obtain family history, to help save my life. And that was the extent of her life that I know, which was not much at all. I wondered if she kept a diary. I'd love to learn more about Great-grandmother.

I approached her closet and opened it. Clothes hung on hangers. A few pairs of shoes rested on the floor, and a blue tote sat on a shelf. I expected the tote to be heavy, but, to my surprise, it was light as a feather. I sat it on the floor in front of me. A terrible feeling washed over me, resonating deep—a warning not to open it.

I stared intently at the tote. My heart pounded as a sharp pain ripped through my skull, and my stomach twisted into a violent cramp. *This can't be good.* I took a deep breath, preparing myself. My hands trembled to unlock the latches on both sides.

A folded piece of paper lay amongst the contents—a box that had been busted open where a lock must have been and two small unfamiliar books. I unfolded the paper.

To My Beautiful Wife,

I am so sorry for what I have done. I cannot live with the guilt a day longer. The guilt has tormented my soul, and I am reminded of how horrible a man I am every time I look at you and our daughter. I never meant for any of this to happen. I met Ashley at work when she was twenty-two and an assistant at the firm, and I eventually gave in to the temptation and couldn't stop my sexual urges. I was not honest with you about being laid off. I resigned after the firm found out about Ashley, since the relationship was considered against company policy. I was very selfish, and I blame myself for everything that has happened. The guilt is eating me alive. I can't eat or sleep. It is completely consuming me. I trusted Joseph to care for our daughter while I slept with another woman against our vows of marriage, and I know this

must hurt you immensely. But, worst of all, the man I trusted raped our daughter for three years and got her pregnant. Even though Joseph was found guilty and is in prison for hurting our little girl, I cannot live with the guilt any longer. I am reminded of the horrible husband and father I am and how neither of you deserved this. So, I am doing what I do best and being selfish by ending the torment eating me alive. I am sorry for everything. You and Natalie will be much better off without me around. You both deserve a better man in your lives. I always loved you, Mary, even if you don't want to believe me. Goodbye.
    Elliott

Oh, my God! Mary's husband had committed suicide. Joseph had raped my father's biological mother. Is that the reason he had been put up for adoption? Why had he never told me about any of this? Did he know? Or had Mary kept this from him too?

I had to know if Great-grandmother had kept more of her life a secret. I reached into the tote and removed an old carved wooden antique box covered in dust. I blew on it as the dust particles danced and swirled into the air before disappearing. I coughed, clearing my throat as an overwhelming feeling of darkness befell me.

I opened the box. A book sat inside—a diary—and in-between the pages rested a folded-up piece of paper. I unfolded it, but the note was in a different language. I set it aside, opened the diary and read the bookmarked entry.

November 3, 1888
    A crazy, old woman approached me on the street in London this evening wearing a hooded long black cloak, claiming I would be punished for marrying Aaron Kosminski and any child born of us, and all descendants thereafter would be cursed and that only an angel born into the family could break it. The crazy woman then handed me

a folded paper, turned and walked away, disappearing into the darkness.

I flipped to the front cover, reading *Margaret Abigail Walker*. Creepy, a curse … And who was Aaron Kosminski? This had got very strange.

A chill ran through me, sending shivers down my spine and making the hairs on my arms stand. I sensed someone in the room with me, watching. I quickly looked behind me but saw no one.

"Is that you, Great-grandma?" I asked in a shaky tone.

No answer came.

I reached into the tote and retrieved two other diary-looking books. I opened the first one. *Madeline Grace Walker* had been handwritten on the front cover, and *Mary Elizabeth Walker* had been inscribed on the other. I skimmed through Madeline's diary and stopped on the last entry.

July 21, 1967

My grandmother, Margaret, handed me an old carved wooden antique box. Something about it felt amiss. It felt wicked, giving me a gut-wrenching feeling. When Margaret handed me the box, she said an angel would be born and would be the only one who could break the curse that has been on this family for generations. I thought Margaret was delusional, so I buried the box far away from my family. But, hours after returning home, it mysteriously appeared on my bed. I was frightened. The box must be possessed. I took it outside and threw it in our firepit and set it on fire. I stood there for several minutes then walked back to the house. Hours later, I peeked outside the window and noticed the fire had stopped smoldering. I walked to the firepit, and there was the box in perfect condition and untouched by the fire.

Could this get any creepier? I set down the diary and opened Mary's, afraid of what I would find. I flipped through the pages until something caught my eye. I stopped and read the entry.

January 11, 2011

Something horrible happened last night. Isabella's close friend, Lindsey, and her entire family died in a house fire in their sleep. I think I made a horrible mistake. I hope I'm just overthinking and he had nothing to do with this, and maybe this was all just a crazy coincidence. But, deep down inside, something doesn't feel right. I know how much Trevor absolutely adores Isabella. It kills him to see her hurt. Isabella and I are close, and she confides in me. She told me that Lindsey has been bullying and humiliating her in front of everyone at school. The only way she feels relief is by cutting herself. I had a little too much wine to drink last night after dinner with Trevor and Isabella. Isabella went to bed early, since it was a school night. And I was very concerned for Isabella and scared she was causing harm to herself and how bad she was hurting inside from her only friend turning on her and humiliating her. Trevor tensed up immediately, and his expression turned dark and disturbing. I'm sure he was upset. He would do anything to protect his little girl. But the poor man has been through a lot in his life. He was adopted and raised by an alcoholic mother, met the girl of his dreams who died during childbirth, raised his daughter alone who, at age five, was diagnosed with cardiomyopathy and needed a heart transplant or she would die. He got his adoption unsealed under the family history medical and safety act in hopes to save his daughter's life, found out that his biological mother was raped and impregnated with twins who were separated at birth and put him up for adoption. His biological mother died in a car accident shortly after he was born. He fell madly in love with a girl who was also involved in a car accident and was in a coma for almost twelve weeks. She lost her memory but regained it back. They get married, had a baby, and she dies during childbirth. After unsealing his adoption, he finds out that his wife is actually his twin sister and is absolutely devastated, finds the only match for his daughter's extremely rare blood type, AB-, and new heart is from the man who had raped and violated his biological mother and was executed after killing two men in prison. And that a curse had been put on our family over a century ago by a London witch who felt the need to punish our family because my great-grandmother, Margaret, had married Aaron Kosminski, aka Jack the Ripper. I've been through a lot, but I think my grandson has been through much more in his lifetime. He will go to the ends of the world to protect his daughter. I really hope that fire was an accident and that Trevor did not start it.

For just a moment, I felt bad for Dad and everything he had endured. I flipped to the last entry in Mary's diary.

May 14, 2023

I finally got the courage tonight to tell Trevor that he could not hide any of this from Isabella any longer, that she was a grown woman and deserved to know the truth about everything, that if he didn't come clean with her, I would. I am scared to death of Trevor. He has a darkness in him that he does a very good job hiding. But, if you trigger his weakness, which is Isabella, he will snap into someone terrifying right before your eyes. This is only the second time I have seen the look in his eyes. Pure evil. It only last for a split second, but it's long enough for me to feel the hatred and the dark in him. He told me that he couldn't do it, that Isabella is very fragile and wouldn't be able to handle the news, and that he's afraid what she might do to herself if she finds out. He tried to make me promise not to say anything, that it was for Isabella's own good, saying that sometimes some things are better off not known. But I couldn't promise him that. We kept these suffocating secrets from her long enough, and it was eating me inside He was very angry with me, threw his glass across the room, and it shattered into pieces. I left immediately, came home and cried in my pillow until I calmed down.

I closed her diary and tried to process all this crazy information as my mind violently twisted into knots. Had my father killed Mary? Had he made it look like she had peacefully died in her sleep, but actually killed her because she had threatened to tell me everything—everything they had kept from me for twenty-three years? For just a moment, I felt bad for Dad, for everything bad he had experienced in his life. But, just as quick as that feeling came, it left, and an overwhelming anger filled every inch of me and made my blood boil.

Had my father killed Lindsey? Had he killed Mary? My head spun as I felt the walls close in on me. My heart hammered in my chest. My head split in two. My stomach twisted painfully as I slowly suffocated from the inside.

THE TAPE

(TREVOR)

"We need to talk," Rachel demanded.

"Okay. What about?" I asked nervously.

"I know you said you didn't want to invade Bella's privacy." Rachel looked away.

"But, with a murder investigation and Isabella being our only lead, I couldn't resist watching the session."

"How could you do that?" I pleaded.

"I wanted to eliminate her as a suspect. We need proof she had no motive. Her breaking in, stealing her file, and her therapist found dead in his office does not look good."

"I know. I know. So, what did you find?"

"You have to watch for yourself." Rachel opened her laptop and clicked on the file.

***

After twenty minutes, the session ended. I sat staring at the screen in shock. This couldn't be happening. This couldn't be true. If Rachel brought this to the police, Isabella would spend the rest of her life in prison or, worse yet, get the death penalty. How had I not seen this? I couldn't lose my baby girl too. I'd already lost too many people in my life. I won't let this happen.

"Are you going to say anything?" Rachel asked, waiting for a response.

"We can't show this to the police."

"We have to. Isabella is a serial killer. She just admitted to killing all those people. But, what I don't understand is, why her therapist didn't bring this evidence to the police."

"Doctor-patient confidentiality."

"Clearly Isabella is the serial killer, and he had a moral right to bring this information to the police immediately."

"Wait. Isabella did society a favor. These people she killed are bad people. They don't deserve to live. Isabella felt the need to give the victims the justice they deserved. If the court system wasn't so corrupt and let these sickos walk free, they'd still be alive."

"That is not Bella's decision. She can't take the law into her hands and take the lives of others."

"The world is better off without them, and now you want to punish Isabella for doing something we all wish we could do to them."

"You can't just go and kill people. It's murder. It wasn't self-defense. It was calculated. She tortured these people. Whether they deserved it or not, she killed people, Trevor."

"At least talk to Isabella. Let her explain herself."

"It doesn't matter. Your daughter is a murderer. I need to make a phone call. Don't worry, I'm not going to the police with this just yet. I need all the answers before I do."

"What kind of answers?"

"Who Carrie really is, and if she has any relation to Dr. Marshall. That'd be the only reason I could see why he wouldn't go to the police with this information and refuse to see Isabella anymore."

"Carrie was Bella's roommate in college. They were best friends. But she got married, had a baby and moved to California."

"You heard the session. Carrie is involved. She helped. She's an accomplice. She must be questioned regarding the murders."

"She lives in California. How can she be involved?"

"Carrie hacked the FBI database and got the files of the victims' court cases unsealed. She's an accessory to murder. Isabella is a very intelligent woman. She could have gotten away with the murders if we hadn't stumbled across this evidence."

"She doesn't have to spend the rest of her life in prison. Isabella needs help. It's not her fault. It's in her blood."

"You aren't making any sense, Trevor. What do you mean?"

"I'm sure you've heard of Jack the Ripper?"

"Of course. Who hasn't?"

"He's my great-great-grandfather. His real name is Aaron Kosminski."

"But he never got caught. No one knows Jack the Ripper's true identity."

"You're right, but they didn't have enough evidence to prosecute him for the murders. But recently they found DNA from a century-old bloodstained scarf linked to one of Jack the Ripper's victims, Catherine Eddowes. Aaron Kosminski was a suspect for many years. Since the scarf had been subjected to contamination for decades, and it's not clear if it had been really left behind by Catherine or her killer, experts claim it's not considered evidence."

"Even if your great-great-grandfather *is* Jack the Ripper, it doesn't give Isabella a free card to go kill a bunch of bad people."

"No. But if the killer instinct is in her genes, then she doesn't need to be punished. She needs to get help. Locking her up isn't going to make the victims come back, but at least we can try to save her. It's not her fault, Rachel. Please don't do this."

"I need to find out more about Carrie. I'll be back. I promise I won't go to the police with this until we talk more. But I need to do this."

OUT OF CONTROL

(TREVOR)

I got a text that Rachel was heading home from the office. I was stir crazy all day, sitting at home by myself with all the demented thoughts that controlled my fragile mind, festering in a break of psychosis and anxiety. I didn't feel right. Something was amiss. How would I protect Isabella? I was torn. I loved my wife, but I loved Isabella even more. She was my daughter; how couldn't I? Life was complicated, and I couldn't believe I was in this absurd situation.

I paced back and forth until I heard Rachel's car pull up the driveway and park inside the garage. I had to calm down. Rachel couldn't see me this way. I tried to calm my nerves by taking slow, deep breaths and counting to ten.

"Hi, honey. I brought home dinner from Giovanni's. Their special tonight was pasta carbonara with freshly baked garlic bread sticks," Rachel hollered as she entered the house.

She waltzed through the kitchen, holding a few bags, flashed a smile and kissed me. She set the bags on the kitchen island and pulled the Styrofoam containers from the bags. She grabbed plates and silverware from the cabinet and served the food.

"Would you mind grabbing a bottle of white wine from the cellar?"

I forced a smile. "Of course."

How could she act as if everything was normal? She had been ready to go to the police and put my little girl behind bars for the rest of her life. This was not okay; my life was ruined.

I scanned all the wine bottles in our massive wine cooler. All our red wines rested on racks, and the whites sat in the cooler. We always chose white wine with pasta, fish, and chicken, and reds with our red meats, like steak and burgers. I found the perfect one for tonight—Domaine d'Auvenay Criots-Batard, a $2,300 bottle of wine. It tasted exquisite. It hailed from a French vineyard, and connoisseurs considered it a delicious and delicate wine and one of the most aromatic.

A moment later, I poured the wine in our glasses and set them on the table.

Rachel smiled. "Great choice, my love. One of my most favorite wines of all." She raised her glass to her lips. "*Mm-mm!* Absolutely phenomenal." She licked her lips.

"Did you find what you were looking for?" I asked.

"I did. Actually, I'm pretty proud of myself, if I say so myself."

"*Aaaand?*"

"Carrie Mitchell, maiden name Carrie Evans, is Dr. Marshall's half-sister from a different father. Carrie Evans married Chad Mitchell and moved to San Francisco and works for the FBI. I haven't figured out why Carrie would help Bella in such heinous crimes. Unless … Isabella blackmailed her. Maybe Isabella has some dirt on Carrie from college that Carrie doesn't want leaked. That's the only conclusion I have that makes any sense."

I listened intently to Rachel as I tried to absorb everything she was telling me. "So, what'll you do with this newfound information?"

"We need to go to the police."

"I can't do that to Isabella. She has bad blood. It's not her fault."

"What are you talking about? She mutilated and murdered several people. She can't get away with such heinous crimes. She must pay for what she has done."

"Putting her in prison won't bring those people back."

"No. But it *will* keep her from killing anyone else."

"That's why we should get her the help she needs. Let's bring her to be mentally evaluated. She shouldn't be punished. She needs help, Rachel. Have you discussed this with anyone else?"

Rachel looked at her feet and shook her head. "Of course not. I understand your need to protect Isabella. She's your daughter, but, with the information I know, I can't just let it slide. The police need to know. The whole state of Virginia deserves to feel safe again. Without a killer behind bars, they'll live their lives in fear. They shouldn't have to move to feel safe."

"But Isabella doesn't deserve to spend the rest of her life in prison for something that's not her fault!"

"Trevor, it *is* her fault. She knows right from wrong. She knows the difference between good and evil. She's an exceptionally smart woman, and she has *killed* people."

"Bad people ..."

"It doesn't matter. And the judge won't care either. Murder is a crime. She took their lives. They'll never see their families again. She took that from them. She doesn't get to make that choice." Rachel slammed her fists on the table.

My blood boiled. My body's temperature rose. I felt like I was suffocating. I needed air. I stormed from the room.

"Trevor, where are you going?" Rachel stood from the table, concerned.

She doesn't understand. I can't get through to her. She'll ruin or lives. I can't let that happen. I must do something about it. I won't let Isabella spend the rest of her life in prison.

I grabbed a hammer from my toolbox. Gripping it, I felt my veins pulsating. *I must protect my daughter.*

The anger inside me boiled over, and I couldn't take it any longer. I returned to the kitchen. Rachel was leaning against the counter with her back to me. I approached her, raising the hammer over my head, and I hit her as hard as I could.

The *crack* echoed violently. Her body fell to the floor and blood sprayed everywhere.

THE VOICES
(BELLA)

I sat frozen in time, my eyes wild. I rocked back and forth. My breathing increased. My heart hammered in my chest as my blood ran rampant through my bulging veins, desperate for release. I stumbled to my feet as the anxiety built. I shambled to the kitchen in a daze. I stopped in front of a mirror. Haunted by my reflection, I regarded a stranger, confused. I didn't know this person staring back at me. A tear streaked my cheek. I wiped it and walked away.

I grabbed a knife from the block and cut the brachial artery on my left forearm. I cut deep; the release felt intoxicating. I watched as the blood poured from my vein and dripped onto the hardwood floor. The feeling was euphoric. I had forgotten how good it felt.

After the euphoria had disappeared, I was left with an overwhelming feeling of betrayal. How could have my own father and great-grandmother hid such secrets from me? Mary had been right; I deserved to know the truth, but my father had killed her. Was my father a killer, just like me?

I recollected my very first kill. It had been a baby bunny. I don't know why I had done it. Actually, I recalled very clearly that a voice in my head had told me to snap its neck.

I don't know why I hadn't questioned the voice. I had just done it, without hesitation. But I remembered the feeling I had afterward. It felt just like when I used to cut myself. It was intoxicating, and every time I did it, the feeling grew more intense and exhilarating. I relished the feeling, and the only way I could feel it was to cut myself or kill something. I became addicted, obsessed. I needed it; I wanted more.

I knew something was wrong with me at any early age. The voices I heard, if I had told anyone, they would have committed me. They would have thought I was some nut case. I had told one person, and she had betrayed me, had humiliated me. I craved the adrenaline rush I got from killing.

I remembered ripping a frog limb from limb when I was just five years old. I had put it in a shoebox and had hidden it in my treehouse, along with a bird. I had cracked its skull with a rock. But I required something more; animals just weren't cutting it anymore. I had gotten mad at a kid in first grade and had jammed scissors into her eye. The screams had made my entire body tingle. I had threatened to kill her family if she told anyone what I had done. The school had investigated the incident, and they had declared it a "running-and-tripping-while-carrying-scissors accident." The family had moved right after the *accident*.

I wasn't sure why I had so much pent-up anger. I needed to find a release. I had vandalized businesses around town late at night. I'd sneak from the house while everyone slept and would take out all my aggression, smashing windows and lights and trashing the place. It would make me feel good. The anger would subside for a few days, but then it would return with a fury. I couldn't control myself. Destroying things hadn't quenched that thirst. What I really craved was hurting someone. I had wanted that rush I had felt after I had stabbed my classmate in the eye. It was nothing I had ever experienced before, and I had wanted more.

I had tried so hard not to listen to the voices in my head when Lindsey had bullied me. She was my friend; I had liked her. But she had gotten out of control, and the voices haunted my thoughts and had become more aggressive; I had to get rid of them. That was when I had snuck into Nicole's house while they slept and had set their Christmas tree on fire. I hadn't realized the fire would spread so quickly. I had only wanted to hurt Nicole, to teach her a lesson, but the fire had accelerated, and the whole house had burned down, with her entire family in it. At first, I had felt horrible, but the feeling had come and gone faster than I could bat an eye. The feeling had been steeped with excitement and pure ecstasy after the voices had told me she had deserved it and that she could never hurt me or humiliate me ever again.

After the fire, I had started to cut myself. It started because I had felt guilty about what I had done. She was my friend. I should have never listened to the voices. I was sick. Something was wrong with me. But, instead of confronting it, I had started to hurt myself instead, punishing myself for what I had done. To my surprise, I had truly enjoyed it. It had felt more like a release than a punishment. If I felt angry, I'd cut myself. If I felt sad, I'd cut myself. If I thought about all the bad things I had done, I'd cut myself. I had become addicted, and I had all the scars to prove it. But no one had known, because I'd wear long sleeves, even in the summer, and I would never go swimming. But, eventually, I had run out of fresh skin. The scars reminded me of all the bad things I had done.

That's when I had found my new hobby—investigating court cases where the victims were shown no mercy. It was a real tragedy. Tragic mercy killings was what I called them. The criminals walked away with just a slap on the hand. They committed heinous crimes and never paid the full price. They needed to suffer. I had the urge to help the poor victims. They deserved justice, and the court system had failed them miserably.

I had become addicted. I couldn't stop. It felt right this time; not just the feeling I got afterward but that I was some sort of vigilante, cleansing the world of evil and giving the victims peace of mind. I had a real purpose in life. It made me feel exonerated for all the shitty stuff I had done, like killed innocent animals and stabbed a six-year-old in the eye just because she had made me mad or killed my friend's entire family in a fire because she had bullied and humiliated me. As good as it felt, somewhere in the back of my mind, I felt a tingle of guilt. And doing society this justice by killing these psychopaths gave me a purpose. They deserved to die.

I never meant to get Carrie involved. She was my best friend, but she had abandoned me. She had moved far away, and I was angry at her for it. The only way I could unseal those cases was from assistance from an inside source—and that was Carrie. She worked for the FBI. But she would never agree to help me kill people, even if they deserved it, so I had to blackmail her.

I knew that her daughter, Chloe, was not Chad's daughter. If I told Chad, it would destroy their perfect little family. Carrie agreed to my request, as long as I never mentioned anything to Chad about what I knew. All I had to do was keep my part of the bargain, keep my mouth shut and my distance from them. She hated me for it. But I didn't care. My need to kill had grown more important than a friend who had abandoned me.

I had promised her the only contact we'd have would be through post mail. And she had made me promise that when I got the information I needed, I had to destroy it immediately, as to have absolutely no evidence to tie her to the murders.

I had agreed.

***

White flashes of light illuminated the dark skies every few seconds. Thunder echoed through town then slowly faded into the distance. As the thunder grew more consistent, the once-scattered raindrops now violently ripped through the night in a downpour and flooded the streets. The constant loudening roar of thunder along with the lightning bolts that ripped through the once-silent night kept me wide awake. I sat at the end of my bed in a hypnotic trance as my tears fell like the rain out my window.

The betrayal ate me alive. I couldn't bear it any longer. The voices in my head became insufferable, telling me to kill him—my own father. I couldn't do it. I loved him. The echo of several voices in my skull drove me insane.

Kill him!

I couldn't take it anymore. The only way to silence them was to comply and kill Dad. I got on my hands and knees next to the loose floorboards and used a prybar to work them free then threw them across the room in a rampage. I reached my arm into the hole and grabbed the machete.

Kill him!

I bolted from the house and into the dark abyss. The downpour drenched my clothes as I walked to Dad's house, anger raging through every vein.

Kill him! Kill him! Kill him!

"*Stop it!*" I screamed at the top of my lungs as a lightning bolt ripped across the sky. I ran. The house was only a few more blocks ahead. A thunderclap startled me as it echoed, the sound ricocheting off anything in its path. My breathing became heavy, my heart hammering in my chest. and my legs felt heavy.

Only a little bit farther …

I approached Dad's gated property and stopped.

Kill him! Kill him!

I pressed the code on the number keypad, and the gates opened. All the lights were off in the house. They must be asleep. I ran to the door and rummaged through my jacket pocket for the keys, and they fell to the ground.

"Pull yourself together," I demanded.

I unlocked the door and pushed through. I was soaking wet but didn't care.

Kill him!

I covered my ears. "*Stop it! Stop it! Stop it!*"

I ran down the hallway to Dad's bedroom.

Kill him!

I slowly opened the door and flinched as it creaked. I couldn't see a thing, so I flipped on the switch.

Dad bolted upright in bed, rubbing his eyes. "Isabella? What are you doing here?"

I raised the machete. With outstretched arms and all my strength, I swung the machete across his neck. My eyes went wild as I shrieked.

The voices stopped.

I dropped to my knees, covered my face and bawled my eyes out. "*He's dead! I killed him!*"

I grabbed the machete with both hands, cupped the end as tight as I could and drove the machete straight through my heart.

E. A. Owen

Twisted Karma Publishing

Tragic Mercy: Book I (2019)

Suffocating Secrets: Tragic Mercy Book II (2019)

Book III
(Coming 2020)

A Reader's Journal (2019) Over 100-pages to keep track of all the books you read, book reviews, favorite books and authors, book wishlist, and more.

Author Website: eaowenbooks.com
Facebook.com/eaowenbooks